Bright Halo Book Publishing

Bright Halo

Episode One:

Melted Memories

Praise for Bright Halo Episode One:

Melted Memories

This is a quick reading YA fantasy book that is well written and thought out by the author. Would recommend if you like fantasy and mystery.
- **Sarah Scott (from Goodreads and Amazon US)**

For a fantasy read, this reads well and quick. Finished in just under an hour. The story has potential, with elements of suspense it gives the reader a chance to wonder what comes next.
- **Madison (from Goodreads)**

This book was outside of my genre but the descriptions were beautiful. I was transported somewhere else, in a magical world where I felt alongside the main character. The little nuggets of suspense were wonderful to follow.
- **Sloane (from Goodreads)**

I really liked the premise of the book and it's world building was easy to follow and well thought out. It has a lot of potential as a short YA Fantasy story. I really enjoyed reading it.
- **Polly (From Goodreads)**

The vibrant colors had me at page one. I really liked crystal as a main character and enjoyed Leo too. So many questions about the hidden past still left unanswered, but it keeps you reading!
- **DIYduo (From Amazon US)**

This book has so much potential and a good plot twist. The world is complex and well thought. If you like fantasy and books like City of Bones I think you will like this one because it has the same vibes to it. Also it's an easy and funny read.
- **Andreea (From Goodreads)**

I loved many of the details that were put into this book! Crystal and Leo have such a platonic bond, and I just can't wait to read more of this series.
- **Mia (From Goodreads)**

Bright Halo Episode One: Melted Memories

Randeletta Howson

Bright Halo Book Publishing

Copyright © 2022 Randeletta Howson

All rights reserved.

The characters and events portrayed in this book are fictitious. Any similarity to real persons, living or dead, is coincidental and not intended by the author.

No part of this book may be reproduced, or stored in a retrieval system, or transmitted in any form or by any means, electronic, mechanical, photocopying, recording, or otherwise, without express written permission of the publisher.

ISBN: 9798818215068

Cover design by: Randeletta Howson
(Edited on Canva and BeFunky.)
Original Photo: © [kharchenkoirina] / Adobe Stock

First Edition Paperback, 2022
Bright Halo Book Publishing, Leicester, UK.

www.brighthalobook.co.uk

For my Mum, who inspires and encourages me with her creativity, talents, and support.

For my Late Grandad, who laughed at everything and found joy in many things.

And for all my wonderful family, friends and people who love and care about me.

RANDELETTA HOWSON

Prologue: Her Mortal Enemy

Seventeen Years Ago…
Mysagi Holt, Kingdom of Enchanta Divine

A silhouette ran through a forest of towering indigo trees and lush lilac grass. The slender figure in a purple cloak pulled down their hood. She was a young woman with dark bronzed skin, inky tousled hair, and sparkly lavender eyes.

She came to a halt.

BRIGHT HALO EPISODE ONE: MELTED MEMORIES

In her arms, she held a newborn girl wrapped in a snowy blanket. The infant had raven ringlets, a caramel complexion, and a cute button nose.

The woman's body became tense when wetness hit the top of her head, and an intense scent of honey filled the air.

Pitter.

Patter.

Golden raindrops drizzled from the misty green sky, and the woman hugged the child close to her chest and bolted off again, protecting her from the harsh rain.

Time was running out.

Moments later, she stood in the middle of the forest and kissed the baby's forehead and cheeks. Electric violet tears cascaded down her face.

She retrieved a white flower necklace from her pocket and placed it on her palm. It gleamed the colours of the rainbow as she hovered it over the newborn's head.

"Keep her safe, let her grow powerful and wise," she chanted. "Bring her majestic hopes and dreams. Make her wishes come true. Bless the mystic divine heir."

The baby glanced at her with curious chestnut eyes. A whirlwind of scarlet red ascended from the waterfall, and she tucked the necklace into the blanket.

"I hope you'll forgive me, my dear darling. Love you

eternally," she whispered. "Farewell, we will meet again one day."

She enclosed the newborn in a giant pink bubble and dropped the baby into the disappearing whirlwind.

Wiping her tears away, she swirled around to see that her mortal enemy had arrived.

Chalky, stone-faced men wearing lime cloaks stared back at her with their hollow, shadowy eyes.

A lanky, broad-shouldered man, dressed in a grey cape, emerged from the group. With a dark, thorny crown planted on his navy mop of hair, he marched over to her.

"You can't escape me, you fool!!" he shouted. "Where did you send the cursed child?"

"It's a secret I shall never tell," she said. "You're not the only one who likes to hide the truth."

"Listen to me carefully. You're making a grave mistake, and there will be deadly consequences if you don't tell me right this instant. Now speak!"

"All that envy and hatred. Are you not ashamed of your hurtful actions?"

"Who are you to question my authority? You are nothing. I seek the truth and I shall find it."

"Kill me first. She is forever protected."

He smacked her around the face. "Silence, you fool! How dare you mock your rightful King?"

BRIGHT HALO EPISODE ONE: MELTED MEMORIES

She gazed up at his cold crimson eyes and smirked. "You murdered innocent people, you monster! You deserve no respect or forgiveness, Kireo! Remember my words. You will regret all you have brought to this sacred land!"

"Your reckless actions only make you suffer. You have already betrayed me twice. I sentence you to heavy punishment for your treachery." He shoved her onto the grass and pointed at her. "Seize her!"

His sinister clan grabbed her and carried her away. She didn't even try to fight back. She had completed her mission, and she knew what would happen next.

Chapter One: The Birthday Wish

Present Day
Leicestershire, United Kingdom

Mum placed a cherry-red sponge cake on the kitchen table and lit the seventeen candles positioned between the frosting and cream.

"Happy Birthday, Crystal. My little girl has grown up so fast. Make a wish, love," she said, sitting across from me.

BRIGHT HALO EPISODE ONE: MELTED MEMORIES

With my eyes closed, I rested my hands on my lap and nodded.

I wish to escape my mum and be free.

I opened my eyes and blew out the candles. The sweet aroma of strawberries and coconut filled my nose. My mum sure knew how to bake.

"Thanks, mum," I said. "The cake is beautiful. I can't wait to have a slice."

"Hold on, darling." She grabbed a sharp knife from the drawer and stared at the padlocked window.

What was she thinking about so deeply? The locks on the windows and doors had always been there. It wasn't anything new.

She snapped out of her trance and came back to the table.

"Hey, are you okay?" I asked, removing the burnt-out candles from my cake, counting them, and putting them in a neat pile on the edge of the table.

Mum cut a few slices of cake. "I'm doing fine, honey. Why?"

"You zoned out for a while. Are you sure?"

"It's nothing. Life is wonderful as usual. Don't worry."

"Okay, let's eat then." There was no point pressing her for answers, and I didn't want an argument on my birthday.

"Wait, let's enjoy the weather," she said.

Mother wrapped two slices of cake in kitchen roll paper and

handed them to me. Then she unlocked the back door with the house key attached to her floral frock.

I followed her into the garden, feeling like a princess with my wavy pink hair and matching fuchsia gown and heels. My birthdays were always an excuse to dress up and not study.

The afternoon sun shined as we strolled on the lawn, munching on cake, and leaving trails of crumbs on the freshly mowed grass. Wandering past the high hedges and railings, we breathed in the sweet countryside air.

It was perfect mother-daughter time until we stopped at the chained-up metal front gate. Fire appeared in the pit of my stomach. There was no freedom from my mother's controlling ways. It was suffocating.

On distressing days, the thought of pushing her, stealing her key, and climbing the fence came to mind. I craved to explore and journey outside my sheltered existence and live as a normal teenager. But I stayed because my life with my mother was all I knew.

She stuffed our used kitchen roll into her dress pocket. "I'm so proud of you, Crystal."

I plastered a smile on my face. "Really? Why?"

"You have been working relentlessly on your studies and painting every day. Was your birthday wish about becoming an artist?"

BRIGHT HALO EPISODE ONE: MELTED MEMORIES

"If I tell you, then it won't come true." If I told her I wanted to leave her behind, it would only break her heart. Sometimes it was beneficial to lie.

"Fine, you don't have to say anything, love."

"What's your wish?"

"Me? I want you to be blissful and safe."

"Is that it? There must be something else."

"No, I just hope your dreams become a reality. You deserve the world, love."

Did she really believe in the words she was saying? She pretended to be my magical fairy godmother, but in actuality, she was my cruel captor.

When we got back into the kitchen, I cut myself another slice of cake and took a bite. There was a sour taste in my mouth from my birthday stroll, and I hoped the sweetness of the cake would make it go away.

"Crystal, I have a present for you." Mother took out a tiny box from her dress pocket and handed it to me. "Hope you adore it."

She watched me as I opened the box. Inside was a white flower necklace with raindrop petals and a purple gem centre. It felt familiar and unknown at the same time as I held it in the palm of my hand. It was the strangest feeling ever.

"I love it!" I said, handing her the necklace. "Can you put it on, please?"

"Sure." My mother stepped behind my chair and clipped on the necklace. "I'm so glad you love it. It is a cherished and priceless family heirloom. It is part of our legacy. So you need to protect it at all costs. My mother passed it down to me and now I'm passing it down to you."

"Wow! I will look after it, I promise." Hopefully one day, I could pass it down to my daughter as well. But it was weird. I had seen the necklace before, but I couldn't remember when or where. "How come you're giving it to me now?"

"There's something I need to talk to you about."

"What's wrong?"

Mother sighed and sat back down. "Well, I'm giving you my necklace for another vital reason. I know what your birthday wishes has been for the past ten years. And now I can make it happen."

"What are you talking about?"

"I should have never kept you in this house, let alone for seventeen years of your life. I can't apologise enough. Really, I'm so sorry, Crystal."

I shook my head. "Please, I don't want to talk about that today. Let me enjoy my birthday."

BRIGHT HALO EPISODE ONE: MELTED MEMORIES

"No, we need to talk. I'm sorry that you had to live this way. But it's time to give you the freedom you need. I can't hold you back any longer. So I decided that I'm sending you to Wonderstate Academy."

My mouth dropped open. "What? I can't just leave. Are you coming as well?"

"No, I will stay here."

"So I have to travel alone? Please don't do this."

"This is what you have always wanted, Crystal. You can study painting and get out into the real world. This is the right thing for both of us. You need independence and freedom to pursue your dreams. Without me holding you back."

Was she a mind reader?

And why would she only bring it up now? If she could see that I was struggling, why didn't she do the 'right thing' years ago?

I leaned forward in my chair. "Why are you doing this now? You have kept me hostage since birth! And now you are planning to kick me out!"

"You do not know what you're talking about, Crystal. I did all this for a reason. I protected you!"

"From what? Please tell me the truth. I need to know. You never talk about my dad or my family. Why has it always only been me and you?"

"Soon, you'll understand. I will tell you all that information at the right time."

"No, I deserve to know where I came from."

"We need to focus on the present. Tomorrow morning, you'll be leaving and beginning a new life. A fresh start. I have already spoken to the headteacher at Wonderstate. His name is Mr Gold, and he is coming to pick you up. So start packing today."

"Are you insane? I ain't going off with some stranger!"

"You're seventeen. It's time to grow up!"

"Great! Thanks for ruining my birthday!" I screamed and lunged out of my chair.

I grabbed the rest of the cake and threw it on the floor. My blood was boiling. How could she do this to me?

"Crystal! How dare you?" She slapped me across the face.

I was speechless. She had never laid her hands on me before. She normally only hurt me with her words. I held my burning cheek and stormed out of the kitchen.

I slammed my bedroom door and pushed my suitcase off my bed. It fell with a thump as I buried my face in my pillow and burst into tears. I should have been ecstatic.

My birthday wish had come true, but I couldn't live without my mother. I had to change her mind somehow.

BRIGHT HALO EPISODE ONE: MELTED MEMORIES

I pulled out my drawing pencils and my latest art book from my study desk and flipped through. Pages filled with watercolour fantasy worlds. On a blank page, I sketched my birthday cake from memory.

I reached for my painting box at the back of my desk, and a blood-curdling scream rang out downstairs.

I sprinted down the stairs, three steps at a time. "Mum! Mum! What's wrong?"

Welcomed by a deafening silence, I paused on the last step facing the hallway. I was about to call her name again, but something didn't feel right.

Tiptoeing through the living room, I picked up a glass vase from the coffee table. It was better to be safe than sorry.

I stood in the kitchen doorway and a frying pan was resting on the floor.

No one was in sight.

Perhaps my mother had left in a hurry. But what was the scream all about?

I paced back into the living room and a masked man dressed in all black was sitting on the sofa. His dark eyes locked on me. I screamed and ran into the kitchen as fast as I could, locking the door behind me.

It was the beginning of a horror movie, and there was no way out. The living room door collapsed onto the kitchen floor.

The masked man stepped inside and advanced toward me. "Your mother is not here. It's me and you now," he said in a robotic voice.

I grabbed a wet knife from the sink. "Stay away from me," I shouted, waving the knife around and splashing water in his direction. "Who the hell are you? What did you do to my mum? What do you want?"

"You don't need to know all the answers to those questions when you're going to die, anyway."

The masked man grabbed my arms and knocked the knife out of my hand. He was muscular and tall, but I couldn't just give up. My life was on the line and so was my mother's.

I reached out for the knife again, but the masked man kicked me in the stomach and punched me in the face. He threw me across the room like a rag doll, and I landed on my hands and knees. The tiled kitchen floor became blurry as a pool of blood dripped out of my mouth.

I lifted my head up and coughed. "No. Please…"

"This is only the beginning of your pain." The masked man raced towards me and stumbled onto the cake-covered floor with a loud thump.

My eyes refocused. An open padlock was lying next to me, and the back door was ajar. I couldn't see it before. Panic and fear had temporarily blinded me. The man must have broken into the house from the back. I had to take my chance to escape.

My whole body ached as I dashed outside. I was home free. I just had to keep moving and find my mother before the masked man awoke. Who knew what he would do next?

I tripped over and landed on the wooden decking. My hands hurt as I pushed myself up, but I didn't have time to think about the pain. I had to survive first. I jumped up and raced to the front of the house. The gate was wide open, and the chain was swinging in the wind. I couldn't believe my eyes.

Had my mother gone to the countryside and forgotten to lock the gate?

Somehow, I had to warn her not to come back to the house.

The masked man marched through the gate and closed it. "You can't escape me."

How did he catch me so fast? No one could move that quickly.

I bent down in the grass and put my hands together. "Please don't kill me. Please," I begged. "Why are you doing this?"

"Your mum should be back soon, then you can both die together."

"What? Why? Please leave my mum alone!"

"But didn't you seek to be free from her?"

How did he know? Even if he had been stalking me and my mum, I had never said it aloud. "Please stop this! What do you want?"

"You'll find out soon enough." The masked man pulled a grey cloth out of his pocket and placed it over my mouth and nose.

I bet he was smirking under his mask, the sicko. Would he do the same thing to my mother?

My throat burned as the toxic smell filled my lungs and I fell limp. I couldn't move or breathe. I struggled to keep my eyes open as I scratched at the masked man's sleeved arms.

Then everything grew pitch black.

BRIGHT HALO EPISODE ONE: MELTED MEMORIES

Chapter Two: Nightmare Night

I woke up on my bedroom floor with a killer headache and a sandpaper throat. A half-moon in the night sky stared back at me through my window. I was in my cotton dressing robe, but I didn't remember putting it on. Had the masked man redressed me? My skin crawled just thinking about it. Hopefully, he had fled before my mother's return.

I tiptoed towards my door and opened it to the biggest shock of my life. Ashy grey smoke drifted inside and my whole body trembled.

I couldn't believe my eyes.

Rampant orange flames were engulfing the walls, stairs, and ceiling. I covered my nose and mouth with my sleeve and crawled across the carpeted landing of smog and heat.

I banged my fists on my mother's bedroom door, but it was locked. The blaze was getting closer and closer.

"Mum, wake up!" I screamed. "The house is on fire! We need to get out of here!"

A slim young man with short blonde hair appeared at the top of the stairs. "Hey, let me help," he said.

"Who are you?"

"Got no time to explain."

"Fine. Hurry." I stepped aside, and he kicked the door open. My mother was lying on the floor with her eyes closed.

I kneeled beside her and felt a faint breath hit my cheek. "Thank goodness. We will get you out of here."

"No, don't move her," the young man said. "Just wait."

"We couldn't just leave her." I held her hand. "Please, we need to save her."

BRIGHT HALO EPISODE ONE: MELTED MEMORIES

My mother's eyes shot open, and blood seeped through her nightgown. "Is that you, Crystal?" She coughed. "You're alive."

"Yes, it's me, Mum."

"You still have your birthday gift, right?"

I lifted my necklace over my robe's collar. "Yeah, I do."

She squeezed my hand. "Listen, the pendant will protect you, so you must keep it safe, no matter what."

I pecked her warm cheek. "Please, I have you to protect me. You can't leave me."

"Crystal, I'm so glad I got to spend my life with you. Never forget the cheerful times."

"You're going to be okay. You can't die."

"Someone is trying to kill you… so leave right now." She closed her eyes, and with her last breath, she said, "I love… you."

"No, mum, you can't leave me! Wake up! Wake up!" I hugged her in my arms as fat, salty tears rolled down my cheeks.

She couldn't be dead. She was the only family I had ever known, and I was alone in the world now. My mind broke into a million pieces.

Behind her body was a cracked and burned padlock. Why were the locks so breakable today?

The young man opened the window and a chilly wind rushed inside. "We need to leave!" he shouted.

"No, she's the only person I have." I kissed my mother on

her forehead. "I won't leave her alone to burn. There's no way. I rather die here myself!"

Heavy footsteps came up the stairs, and the door swung open. The masked man stared at me as he entered the room. "Finally awake?" he asked. "You slept better than a baby."

I screamed and guarded my mother's body. "Stay away from us! You killed her!"

"And why would I do that?"

"Because you're a monster!"

The masked man grabbed my wrists. "Don't you want to join your mother?"

"Stop it! Why are you doing this?" I screamed, trying to free myself from his icy hands.

"You don't need to know who I am. You just need to come with me. This is your fate!"

"Let go of me!"

"Your mother and you are marked, and I will never let you go." He scratched the back of my right hand. "Never forget that."

I winced at the sharp pain and grew lightheaded as my blood dripped onto the floor.

"Hey, leave her alone!" The young man kicked the masked man and pulled me towards the open window.

Everything was happening too fast as the masked man lifted

my mother over his shoulder and bolted out the door.

Ferocious fire swept through the room and the wall collapsed and caved in. I couldn't even chase after them. They were long gone.

"No! Where is he taking my mum?" I shouted. "We have to stop him."

"The house is going to blow! We must leave now! She wouldn't want you to die. Come on!" the young man said.

He lifted me onto his back and took a supernatural leap out of the window. Who the hell was this guy, and where was he taking me?

Landing in the front garden, he let me down, and we bolted out of the gate and down the pebbled path.

I took one last glance at the house I called home as the fire took over and burned it down. How could my life be destroyed in one night? My mum's body was stolen, and I couldn't do anything to rescue her. I had to find out the identity of her murderer, even if it killed me. I owed it to her.

It was my first time outside the gates, and I had never imagined leaving the house in such a traumatic way. The moonlight guided us through countryside fields and dusty roads. My life was over and there I was, following a stranger into the dark.

Why did the masked man kill my mother? And why didn't he

kill me when he had the chance? I couldn't get his evil eyes out of my mind.

"Where are we going?" I asked, trying to keep up with the young man's swift pace.

"Into hiding, of course." He pointed to a car in the distance. "Should only take two hours to get there, and then we can figure out a plan from there."

"Why are you helping me? What's in it for you?"

"I couldn't just leave you behind, could I? We need to escape as far as possible from here."

"But I don't even know who you are."

Before I could finish my sentence, he said, "My name's Leo and whatever you do, don't look back."

BRIGHT HALO EPISODE ONE: MELTED MEMORIES

Chapter Three: Tearful Raindrops

*I*t was dark outside the passenger's window, as raindrops descended the glass endlessly, resembling the tears on my face. A mute, choked-up cry that left me breathless. There was nothing I could do to bring my mum back. It was the worst day of my existence. My salty tears fell into the deep cut on my hand, and it strung, but I didn't care. It was ironic: I had no burns from the fire, but the masked man gave me a physical and emotional scar.

I wanted to rewind time as I cradled my mum's necklace in my hands. It wasn't a perfect life, but at least I would be with her. Alive, cheerful, and safe.

Leo drove without saying a word. The silence was deafening. I only knew his name. So I had to stay alert and hope he was a trustworthy person.

I sniffed and rubbed my sore eyes. "Where are we going?"

"Somewhere secure," he replied. "We'll be there soon."

"But how do I know I can count on you? How did you enter my house?"

"I saw the smoke and the front door was open, and you know what happened next. I couldn't allow innocent people to die. I had to do something."

"But we're in the middle of nowhere. Why were you wondering out there? It makes no sense."

"Why does it matter? It's a free country," he said. "I'm glad I was there to get you out of there."

Why was he so defensive? Anybody else would ask questions. He was making me extra suspicious of him. Did he have a hero complex or something? Who randomly runs into house fires?

"Don't get me wrong. I'm thankful you were there to save

me," I said. "It was extremely dangerous, so seriously, thank you."

I wished he had arrived sooner. How could life be so unfair? Why was I the only survivor? I hoped the murderer had enough respect to bury my mother's body. But I knew I was asking too much from a literal monster.

Leo stopped on the side of the road and handed me a glass bottle from the glove compartment. "Here, drink this. You must be thirsty."

I drank the water, soothing my dry throat. "Thanks."

"Quit thanking me. I helped because I wanted to do it."

"But why?"

"You don't need to know that yet." He retrieved a plaster from his backpack. "Just let me, okay?"

I nodded and held my wounded hand out. He put the plaster on my wound and my pain melted away. My heart raced. There was electricity between us as he touched my skin. I hadn't felt that way before.

Guilt washed over me.

My mother had died and there I was, crushing on a complete stranger. My first crush, in fact.

I coughed and asked, "Why did he kill her?"

"I wish it had ended differently. If only I had got there sooner and stopped him," Leo said, speeding down the road.

"It isn't your fault. The only person I blame is the intruder. I still don't understand why he killed my mother and took her body. She didn't deserve to die. Where do you think he is now?" I knew my mother would want me to be safe. But I was a horrible daughter for not chasing after the masked man.

"No idea. He is fleeing. But, if he has other ideas, he could find you if I let you out. I know you don't know me yet, but please try to trust me. I will get you somewhere safe. It's the least I can do."

"I want to believe you, but I can tell you're hiding the truth, so please tell me. Why were you really there?" I asked.

For an unknown reason, I felt safe around him, and like I had known him forever, but I couldn't get too comfortable and let my sudden stupid feelings take over. I needed to stick to logic and stay focused.

"It's a long story, Crystal," he said. "I will explain later."

"I need to know now. Please tell me."

The car stopped, and Leo let go of the steering wheel. "You got to be kidding me!"

"What's wrong?"

"Something's up with the engine."

"What are we going to do?"

"We are far away from your house. We'll be fine and I'll be quick. Don't worry, okay?" He grabbed a torch from under his seat and stepped outside the car.

I drank the rest of the water and accidentally dropped the bottle behind Leo's seat. It had landed on a suspicious briefcase. I put the bottle in my pocket and placed the briefcase on my lap. I didn't want to be nosy, but I had to know what Leo was hiding. So I clicked it open and inside were stacks and stacks of cash. My mouth dropped open.

Why would he have all this money?

Was he a hitman or a conman?

There was a loud knock on the car window. I dropped the briefcase back behind Leo's seat. It was no time to panic. I had to act normal. I slipped out into the rain with the empty glass bottle in my hand. "Leo, you can't scare me by knocking on the door."

Leo closed the car bonnet. "I didn't do anything."

"But I heard you, so stop lying to me."

"Why would I?"

"I don't know. Perhaps you enjoy playing mind games."

"If you want to survive, don't move." He grabbed the bottle out of my hand and smashed it on the road.

"What are you talking about?"

"Just do as I say."

"Stop messing about!"

"Stay completely still." He pulled out a knife, picked up the neck of the shattered bottle, and threw them both towards me.

I screamed and ducked. "What the hell are you doing?"

"Why did you move?" he asked, with no expression.

My heart was racing when I stood up. "Are you serious? You could have killed me!"

"Calm down," he said, pointing behind me. I twisted my head and there was a masked man in a grey suit on the road with the knife buried in his chest.

"Is that him? The killer?" I asked, feeling shivers run down my spine and anger in the pit of my stomach.

"No clue, but we need to get out of here now!" Leo shouted, darting towards the car.

"What about my mother's body?"

"He is already dead, and her body is nowhere in sight, so let's leave."

I followed him, hiding my shaking hands behind my back. Even if I attempted to run away, he would have chased me and caught me in a second. He killed the stranger with ease, and my mind was breaking.

Too much pain.

Too much death.

Too much grief.

Then the man took a deep breath.

BRIGHT HALO EPISODE ONE: MELTED MEMORIES

Leo yanked the knife out of the unknown man's chest and used it to cut open the man's white shirt. If I hadn't seen the killer with my own eyes, I would certainly have suspected Leo. I had to trust him for now, and if he wanted me dead, he would have left me in my burning house.

"How is he still alive?" I asked.

"He's wearing a bulletproof vest," Leo said, taking the mask off the man; green eyes and a brown beard were hidden underneath.

The man moaned in pain. "Help me."

Was this the guy who murdered my mum? He could have easily replaced the black clothing, so I couldn't rule him out.

Leo picked up the man's gun and pointed it at him. "Who are you, and why did you try to kill us?"

"What are you talking about?" the man asked, looking up at Leo. "Are you crazy?"

"Don't play dumb! We caught you holding a gun and wearing a mask."

"I believed Crystal was in danger, and I was trying to protect her."

"How do you know her name? Who are you?" Leo asked. He had taken the words right out of my mouth. "I will give you one minute to answer."

"My name is Mr Gold," the man said.

I took a step toward them. "Your name is Mr Gold?"

Leo interrupted me. "Stay back!"

I ignored his warning and continued. "Did you kill my mum? She said you were going to visit us tomorrow."

"Of course not," Mr Gold replied. "Wait, she is dead? I'm so sorry… She wanted me to take you back to Wonderstate Academy with me."

"Crystal's not going anywhere with you. This man is lying for all we know," Leo said.

He sure had a terrible temper, but I could understand how he felt. It was a foolish idea to get on his bad side, but I had to stick up for myself.

"No, he's telling the truth," I said. "And my mum mentioned him and Wonderstate Academy today. I trust him."

"Are you insane? He could be the killer," Leo said. "This could have been his plan all along."

"Well, what else are we going to do?"

"I don't know. Get rid of him, I guess."

What had I got myself into? I was alone with two strange men, and I didn't know who to trust. I had to tread carefully.

"Please, Leo, what if he is innocent?" I begged. "We need to take this chance, okay? I have nothing left to lose now, and my mum wanted me to go to Wonderstate. It was her last wish."

Leo shook his head. "Fine, he doesn't look honest to me, so

BRIGHT HALO EPISODE ONE: MELTED MEMORIES

don't say I didn't warn you, but I won't let you go alone, so get the first aid kit in the back."

I raced to the car and came back with a green medical box. "Here."

Leo took the large glass fragments out of Mr Gold's leg with tweezers and wrapped bandages around the wound. His hands were still and precise.

"Now get up," he said, pulling Mr Gold up from the ground. "If you're telling the truth, we need to know where your school is."

"It's in the centre of London, fifteen Redford Drive," Mr Gold replied, limping towards the car.

"This better not be a trap."

"I assure you it isn't. If someone is after you, I can enrol you both in Wonderstate to keep you safe. It would have been what Melander wanted."

Leo clicked his car key, and the car boot popped open. "We will see when we get there. Get in the boot or else," he commanded, still holding the gun at Mr Gold.

"Why are you acting this way?" I asked. "He is trying to help us."

"We don't know his actual intentions, and I ain't risking it."

"I don't know your intentions, either."

Mr Gold lifted himself into the car's boot. "It's fine. I have nothing to hide."

"Let's get moving," Leo said, closing the car boot. "Hopefully, he survives the ride."

"Are you sure we should do this?" I asked as we proceeded to the front of the car.

"He tried to kill us."

"But-"

"We have no choice, so let's go. If he is telling the truth, he will be fine. Let's get out of here now."

We got into the car, and I couldn't stop trembling in my seat. Leo threw the medical kit on the back seat and then drove off. His facial expression was blank as the faint sound of banging from the boot of the car died down after five minutes. The silence was deafening. Was Mr Gold still alive?

I couldn't help but imagine me and Leo in a courtroom in handcuffs, with a judge knocking his gavel and shouting the word, 'GUILTY!' I was fairly sure putting someone in a boot at gunpoint counted as kidnapping. It was wrong. I was a coward, and I did nothing to stop Leo.

We were now partners in crime.

BRIGHT HALO EPISODE ONE: MELTED MEMORIES

Chapter Four: Perfect Charade

One Year Later...

In art class, I swirled my paintbrush in the palette of colours, adding the last elements to my painting. It was a portrait of a woman with chocolate-brown eyes, dark wavy hair, and high cheekbones. It was the only image I had of my mother in my brain.

The house fire destroyed everything but my memories. My project was practically completed, but the details of long, curly eyelashes and trimmed brows were missing.

Mrs Elson, our teacher, clutched her handbag from her desk and removed her round glasses. "There's an urgent issue that I must resolve. I will be fifteen minutes. Continue on your projects, class," she said, before rushing out of the classroom and closing the door.

The room erupted into chatter and noise. Some students continued to work, while others gathered and gossiped.

After collecting felt-tip pens from the corner drawer, I bumped into Kelly.

She spun around, hit me in the forehead with her auburn ponytail, and glared at me with her grey eyes. "Look what you have done, you idiot?"

There was a massive black line across her drawing of a sandy beach and an orange sunset.

I gasped. "Oh no, I'm so, so sorry."

"You did it on purpose!"

Our classmates surrounded us in matching white shirts and purple blazers. We wore the same uniform, but I didn't belong. Even after 360 days of attending Wonderstate, I was an outsider and Kelly would never allow me to forget that.

BRIGHT HALO EPISODE ONE: MELTED MEMORIES

I stepped back. "I said sorry."

"Is that all you have to say? You ruined my assignment!"

"You should be able to blend it in. I can show you how."

"Nobody needs your help. You suck. You should worry about yourself." She moved closer to me.

"Get out of my face!" I shouted.

She snickered. "No, stop being a crybaby."

The class of students cheered. "Fight! Fight!"

Leo stood between Kelly and me, and the room grew quiet. He shook his head at her. "Why don't you leave Crystal alone?"

She scowled at him. "Why are you sticking up for her? We all know she's a loser."

"Why? Unlike you, she doesn't act as if she is better than others. Just let it go."

"Stop embarrassing yourself. She isn't as sweet as she pretends. She is fake."

Leo's captivating blue eyes looked sorrowful for me, and I hated it. "She already apologised, and it was clearly an accident," he said. "The only fake person here is you."

I pushed past him and stared at Kelly. "I'm not scared of you and nothing's gonna change that."

"Watch me." She grabbed a pot and threw red paint across my art piece.

"I'm going to kill you!" I screamed, trying to punch her, but

Leo held me back. "Take your hands off me!"

He gripped me tighter. "Come on. Chill out." I tried to wriggle free from his grip, but he was way too strong.

The students started laughing and shouting. I couldn't hear my own thoughts.

Kelly giggled. "You're such a joke!"

The class fell silent when the door swung open, and Mrs Elson marched into the classroom.

She pointed at me and Kelly and yelled, "You two, go to the headteacher's office now!"

Who knew waiting outside the headteacher's office on a leather chair would be its own form of torture? It had only been ten minutes, but it felt like forever sitting next to my mortal enemy.

"What is your problem?" I asked, breaking the awkward silence. "I don't understand you at all."

Kelly frowned. "You ruined my painting and now you are acting all innocent. But I can see right through you, and I will make sure Mr Gold knows, too."

"Come on. You know it was an accident. You ruined mine on purpose."

"Whatever, you're a liar. I don't even know why Leo sticks up for you. It's mortifying."

BRIGHT HALO EPISODE ONE: MELTED MEMORIES

"Are you jealous or something?"

"Seriously, you'll never be on my level. I could never be jealous of you."

The headteacher, Mr Gold, stepped out of his office. "That's enough. Let's discuss this inside."

Kelly pushed in front of me as we followed him inside and he parked himself behind his desk as we sat across from him.

He took out two folders from his drawer. "So, would you please explain what happened? I'm extremely disappointed."

Kelly admired her manicured nails. "Crystal destroyed my artwork on purpose."

"That's not true!" I said, shaking my head.

Mr Gold leaned forward in his chair. "One of you is lying, so come clean or you will both get detention."

"What?" I and Kelly said in unison.

"You both are outstanding students normally, and your art pieces are due to be graded in a week," Mr Gold said.

"Well, I'm telling the truth," Kelly said. "I have nothing else to say."

"Detention for the rest of the week, then," Mr Gold replied.

"My father won't be pleased about this unfair treatment." Kelly got her phone out of her pocket and started typing.

She thought she owned the world. This was just another reason to hate her, and the list was growing.

Mr Gold sighed. "Fine, I'm giving you both a verbal warning, but I can't extend your deadline for your art pieces."

Kelly smirked and put her phone away. "That's fair and understandable, sir."

Mr Gold nodded. "You may leave, Kelly. Crystal, can you stay for a brief chat?"

Kelly smiled and strode out of the office. "Bye. Thank you, sir."

Of course, she didn't care about art. The only thing she cared about was her daddy's money and the status it gave her.

I put blood, sweat and tears into my piece and I knew my mother would have been proud of how far I had come. It was unfair.

I sighed. "So she gets away with it yet again. I'm so tired of her."

Mr Gold stood up. "Look, I believe you, but we have to be careful. Don't worry about her. She has her own issues, and it has nothing to do with you. I will talk to her and sort it out."

"I have been trying to ignore her, but Kelly keeps starting on me all the time."

"How are things going otherwise? Is Leo still looking after you? Have you found out anything about your mother yet?"

"No, I haven't, and Leo says it's too dangerous to dig into my past right now, but I can't just sit around and do nothing."

BRIGHT HALO EPISODE ONE: MELTED MEMORIES

"I think he's right. Are you sure you want to know?" He paused and tapped his desk with his fingers. "We don't know who she was or what she was hiding. She must have hidden it for a reason. I mean, perhaps the truth is too much to handle."

"If I don't understand my past, I don't know me. Even if it's traumatic, I need to know. I can't pretend she didn't exist."

"Melander was a kind person, so I will help however I can. I just feel ashamed that I haven't been able to find any information for you yet."

"It isn't your fault. No matter what, I will find out the masked man's identity myself and I will make him pay for his crimes."

I spoke bravely, but I didn't know how I would cope if I had to face him again. If I were honest with myself, I would probably run and hide and have a panic attack.

Mr Gold put his hand under his chin. "I understand how you feel, but the masked man wouldn't be easy to take down if he crops up. I'm worried about the consequences."

It was already too late. The unthinkable had already happened. I couldn't even piece together my past with my murdered mother. But by consequences, I knew Mr Gold meant that the masked man could kill me next. But if I thought about that too much, I would drive myself crazy.

"Well, don't worry about me, sir. I will be fine," I said. "Are you planning to extend the project deadline or not?"

"I can't. It's impossible to do an excellent piece, similar to the other students in three days. It's not fair to you. We can set something up in two weeks."

I stood up from my chair. "Two weeks? I don't want to get behind when I worked so intensely all year. So I'm determined to finish my art piece on time. I will get it done by Friday."

"You need to calm down, Crystal," Mr Gold replied. "Gracious speech, but it's not that serious. I won't let you fail your class."

"My mother sent me here for a reason."

"I know, but she would want you to be smiling and to stop stressing yourself out. It's okay to be behind. You will catch up. You're talented."

"Whatever, you and Leo don't understand. Telling me what to do all the time. I'm sick of it." I picked up my handbag and left his office.

The white mansion of Wonderstate Academy shaded me from the sun. I was sitting on a bench in the middle of the courtyard. The soothing sound of water from the wildflower-covered water fountain filled my ears and calm washed over me. I smiled to myself and closed my eyes.

BRIGHT HALO EPISODE ONE: MELTED MEMORIES

When I opened my eyes, Leo was sitting next to me. He glared down at me and asked, "Hey, you alright?"

I sat up on the bench. "When did you get here?"

"Just now. I didn't mean to scare you. What did Mr Gold say? Did he give you detention?"

"No. We got verbal warnings. Kelly is getting away with it because her father is rich. So unfair."

"I know. Even Mr Gold fears her at this point. Money rules the world, I guess."

"Yeah, it sucks. Someone has to knock Kelly off her high pedestal."

"I'm sorry about your painting and Kelly, but you're drawing way too much attention to us. You need to act normal and let it go."

He didn't understand what I was suffering through; grief, bullying, and hiding from a murderer. I wish I could switch off my feelings and emotions, but I couldn't. I would wake up in the morning and I would feel okay at first. But then I would remember that night of the house fire and my blood would run cold.

I folded my arms. "Normal? I don't even know what that means. I don't think I can do this any longer. Even Kelly can see that I'm a freak."

"Who cares what she thinks?"

"It's easy for you. People naturally likes you. It's a different story for me. I wish I could just blend in."

He placed his hand on my shoulder and softened his voice. "Just be careful, okay? I'm trying to help you."

I shook my head. "No, you're trying to watch me and control my every move. I don't have to do what you say. I want to be left alone."

The bell rang, and students poured out from their classrooms and into the courtyard, and Leo removed his hand from my shoulder.

Kelly strode past with a group of girls. She said something, and they all laughed as they left through the front gate.

I sighed. "She is obviously talking about me. I can't stand her."

Leo shook his head. "Ignore her. Stop letting her control you."

"Yeah, you're right. And I need to stop letting you control me as well, right? Or are you planning to be a hypocrite?"

"Is that what you think? I'm not trying to control you."

"But you are always telling me what to do! You are the same as Kelly."

"No, it's different. I'm not a bully. I'm just trying to-"

"Trying to help? Well, you can do that by leaving me alone." I took my escape before he could say another stupid word.

BRIGHT HALO EPISODE ONE: MELTED MEMORIES

I was tired of him acting like he was the angel and devil on my shoulders. Why did every person in my life want to control me? Originally, it was my mother, and now it was him.

As I stepped into the academy's entrance, I glanced at Leo. He was still sitting on the bench, staring down, and his eyes were watery. He seemed just as lost and lonely as me.

Chapter Five: Tell Me Everything

*A*fter a long day of lessons, my head was spiralling out of control. How would I complete the art project by the due date? It was impossible to finish by the end of the week. It took weeks to paint the original. But I had to get it gone and prove Leo, Mr Gold, and Kelly wrong. I needed to become an artist and make my mum proud. Nobody understood me. It was a useless assignment and a burden for them.

However, to me, it was my passion and dream. And my mother's wish.

I returned to my halls of residence and my roommate, Amber, was lying on the living room sofa, watching a murder mystery show. Her latest obsession.

When I slammed the front door shut, she switched off the TV. "Crystal! Tell me all the gossip," she said. "People were talking about how Leo saved you from Kelly. And that you were super close in the courtyard. Is it true?"

I sat next to her, throwing my backpack under the coffee table. "Kill me now."

"At least you had an interesting time. So jealous. I had boring double maths, and someone farted in the dining hall."

Amber's days sounded normal and calm, and mine were dramatic and stupid. I would've done anything to swap my life for hers. She has a normal family and a privileged background. While I had the opposite. Alone and traumatised.

I laughed. "Gross. Had no lunch today." I lost my appetite after the day's arguments. I only drank a glass of water in the morning.

"Believe me, I didn't eat after that fart. It stunk to high heaven!"

"Was it that awful?"

"Yeah, the person needs to visit a doctor as soon as possible."

"Oh, my gosh. I bet they were embarrassed to death."

"They should be. Hey, I don't want to cook. Do you want pizza? Pineapple and mushrooms, right?"

"Sure, I'm down. You remember everything, don't you?"

She pulled out her phone from her nightgown. "Of course, I do. You're my best friend. Gonna order it."

After three large slices of pizza, five smoked chicken wings, and half a bottle of Pepsi, Amber asked me a question I wasn't expecting. "So, Leo told me your birthday is on Saturday? Were you hiding it from me?"

"No. Just another day init," I said, rubbing my tummy and falling into a food coma.

"Not true. You only turn eighteen once."

"It's fine. I don't want to make a huge thing out of it."

"We need to celebrate it. Please let me organise something."

Leo's giant mouth always got me into trouble.

There was no stopping Amber now.

I learned that the tough way when I moved into Wonderstate Academy. I refused to leave the flat for months, devouring takeaways in my room and crying myself to sleep.

BRIGHT HALO EPISODE ONE: MELTED MEMORIES

Nothing mattered.

I was empty inside after my mother died. I avoided classes, Leo and the outside world like the plague. Luckily, Mr Gold was understanding and gave me a chance to mourn.

One afternoon, Amber came into my bedroom and ordered me to get dressed. I felt guilty for ignoring her, so I forced myself out of bed. We giggled while shopping and carrying plastic bags around town. We relaxed in a Korean BBQ restaurant and shared pork belly over a grill and sipped glasses of coke. That's when she said we would be best friends. I had never had a friend before. But she kept her word, and the rest was history.

"Can we just leave it?" I asked. "Next topic, please. Let's talk about you instead."

"No, you can't shake me off. You deserve a wonderful birthday."

"Fine. You win. I'm going to bed now. Night," I said, escaping into my bedroom.

I pulled out my mother's necklace from my desk drawer, and I wanted to cry. Of course, I didn't want to celebrate my next birthday. Yeah, I would be eighteen and be seen as an *adult*.

But it would also be the anniversary of my mum's death. I didn't even get the chance to pay my respects and bury her.

How could I celebrate when I didn't even know her fate?

I wanted to visit my old house to find a clue, but Leo said it was a horrible idea. I knew he was right; it would only bring further trauma, misery, and regret.

My house would be an enormous pile of ashes by now.

I put the necklace back in the drawer and disappeared into bed.

Out of sight, out of mind.

The heat kissed my skin as I strode through a lake of fire and saw my mother drowning in flames.

Her deafening screams filled my ears, and ashes engulfed me. I dived into the lake and swam towards her.

I pulled her back up to the surface. "What happened to you?" I asked.

"You already know the answer, but you just refuse to admit it to yourself. Am I truly your mother, or am I just a figment of your imagination?"

"Of course, you're my mother. I have memories of you. I spent my life with you."

"Memories are created, manipulated, and deleted. Can you be truly sure?"

"Yeah, I can be. What are you even talking about?"

She combed my hair with her fingers. "I'm saying that it's time to remember the truth. The person you trust the most hides the most secrets. Be brave. You must recover your true self by your next birthday."

BRIGHT HALO EPISODE ONE: MELTED MEMORIES

"And if I don't?" I asked. "What will happen?"

"You won't want to find out." She held me by the shoulders and pulled me down into the lake.

I woke up screaming, drenched in sweat, and my bedsheets were on the floor. The nightmare felt so real. Was my mother really talking to me through the dream world?

I checked my phone to see that I had missed my three alarms. And there was a text message from Leo that read, 'We still meeting today? 10 am?' and I replied 'Yes, of course. See you in an hour.'

Dashing out of bed, I jumped into the shower. As the hot, steaming water drizzled over my body, I knew what to do.

My birthday was a couple of days away and no matter what, I needed to find out what really happened to my mother.

Leo knew something and I could no longer stay in the limbo of not knowing the truth.

Chapter Six: Show A Little Mercy

I was sitting alone in Mercy's café on the outskirts of the city. The aroma of fresh bread rolls, salty chips, and hot coffee filled the air. People were eating breakfast, and chatting across tables, relaxing on coral plastic chairs, while servers paced around on the chequered floor with notepads and pencils.

BRIGHT HALO EPISODE ONE: MELTED MEMORIES

I stared outside the window at the pastel blue sky and the autumn trees of intense red, vibrant yellow, and bright green. The building was higher than ground level, so the sides of human heads bopped past the bottom of the glass.

Leo came through the door and sat on the seat opposite me. "No one followed you, right?" he asked. "Did you see anyone suspicious?"

I glanced at my phone. "Of course not."

"Good, but make sure you check. You never know who could be watching. Also, I'm sorry for being late."

"It doesn't matter. You're here now."

"Wait, before I forget. Here." He pulled out a white, thick envelope from his coat pocket and handed it to me. "Don't use it all at once."

I opened it to discover a stack of cash. "Thank you," I replied, putting it in my handbag.

Without Leo, I wouldn't be alive or living this comfortable lifestyle. He must have been using the money from the mysterious briefcase.

When we arrived at Wonderstate Academy, he brought me a touchscreen mobile phone and a watercolour painting set. I quizzed him about where he got his funds from, and he said he ran away from his rich family. Of course, I didn't believe him, but when he offered me a weekly payment, I accepted it because I had no other choice.

I sipped from my plastic bottle of water. "So, I will get straight to the point. I want you to tell me the whole lot. What really happened to my mum? You must have found out something by now?"

"No idea," he said, picking up the menu. "I'm still looking into it, so be patient, okay? It takes time."

"No, it's ridiculous. It has been a year. I demand to be kept in the loop."

"There is nothing to say. I'll inform you when I learn something."

"We could try to find my family. My mother did say my necklace was a family heirloom. My grandmother gave it to her. She could still be alive somewhere. I have to meet her somehow."

I wished I had brought my necklace with me. It would have been the perfect way to put my point across. But even he could understand the value of family and connections.

"We have talked about this before," Leo said. "There is no information on your family history."

"But they must be out there," I replied. "What if my father is out there looking for me? He must know I exist?"

"We have no information on him, either. It's all complete dead ends. Even with your DNA test, we found nothing. I don't want to get your hopes up again."

"I know, but there has to be something else we can try. Are you even still searching for the masked man? I'm done waiting around. If you don't help me, I will find out for myself, and you can't stop me."

He leaned over the table. "Don't be stupid, Crystal. The masked man is out there. Do you have a death wish or something?"

I sighed. "Okay, okay, I won't do anything, but I wish you would talk to me."

He was always so quick to shoot me down. At least I tried to speak to him. If he couldn't cooperate, I had to help myself. He was absolutely hiding something from me. I could feel it.

"I'm here for you. We have to focus on what's in our control. Have you started your project yet?"

"No, I haven't. I have a lot on my mind, okay? You know, it's the anniversary of my mother's death in a few days."

"Yeah, I understand. I really do, but you told Mr Gold you were determined to complete it."

"So what? I still have time. Why do you care so much?"

"Because I know art is your passion, so you should push yourself and get it done. That is what your mother would have wanted."

"Don't tell me what she wanted. You didn't even know her. I can sort my own life out myself, so butt out. You are so annoying. I will be right back," I said, before sneaking off.

How dare he lecture me?

Yeah, the art project was essential, but finding out what happened to my mother was my main priority. My nightmare was an omen. I couldn't ignore it.

A tall, slim waitress glared at me like she had seen a ghost. "What are you doing here?" she asked.

"I could ask you the same thing."

"Okay, you got me."

It was Amber, my roommate. But not normal designer Amber. She was wearing a black shirt dress and a red apron with a logo of a white outline of a cupcake with a cherry on top.

She scanned the room and pulled me behind the counter, out of the customer's view. "You can't tell anyone, okay?" she begged. "Do you know what they would say if they found out that I worked in this dump?"

"I thought you didn't care what people thought. You sound ridiculous. Kelly and the others would be proud. Listen to yourself."

She gave me sad puppy dog eyes. "I know it sounds terrible, but please promise me you won't say anything. This would be social suicide."

What was the massive deal, anyway?

It was just a normal job in a normal café. But I knew how

harsh people would be if they knew that perfect little rich Amber worked. She had her family's wealth, so why would she need employment? Nothing made sense. I guess every person had their own secrets to hide.

"Crystal, are you even listening?" Amber asked. "Please don't tell anyone about this."

"Sorry, yeah, I promise I will keep it a secret, but you must have known that someone would see you. You're lucky that it was only me."

"No one ever comes here, and if they do, I hide." She scanned the room again and pointed at Leo. "By the way, what are you doing here with him, anyway?"

"It's not what you think. You can't tell anyone that you saw us together."

"Don't worry. I have your back. Good luck with whatever you're doing with him."

"It's nothing weird. We're just friends."

"Sure, whatever you say. I have to get back to work. I will see you later," she said, taking her chance to escape.

I revisited my seat and remembered why I had got up. I had forgotten to ask for service. Amber had distracted me with her problems.

Leo raised his eyebrows. "Where did you go?"

"I can't believe I forgot. My mind is all over the place." I held my head in my hands.

"Is there something you want to tell me?" he asked.

"Well, there is something."

"Spit it out already."

"Amber saw us. She works here."

"What? Your big mouth friend?"

My blood boiled. "I'm sick of you. You're so rude and condescending. You're the one who told her about my birthday."

"Crystal. Chill out. Such a drama queen."

"Oh, am I?" I grabbed my glass and threw the water in his face and over his white t-shirt.

"Are you crazy?" He stood up from his chair and wandered off.

People watched and stared at me, but I didn't care. Leo went into the men's toilets and left his jacket behind on his chair. I knew what I had to do. I fished his jacket over the table and took his spare key.

There was no time to waste. I had to find out what he was hiding from me. I needed the truth.

My hand trembled as I put the key in Leo's boarding room door and twisted it. The hallway was empty and there was no one in sight. I put the key back in my pocket and stepped inside.

BRIGHT HALO EPISODE ONE: MELTED MEMORIES

I had never been in a boy's bedroom before. A musky smell hit me as I nearly tripped over the dirty clothes on the floor. I guess he wasn't as flawless as he seemed. His neat bed conflicted with the clutter everywhere else. But I didn't have time to judge and there was no turning back now.

I had a mission to find out what he was hiding. I drew my eyes to his desk, and I rummaged through the drawer of assignments, chocolate wrappers, and highlighter pens. Nothing out of the ordinary.

I moved all the items onto the top of his desk and found a medium-sized box hidden at the bottom of the drawer. There was neat, curly handwriting on the top of it that read, 'Give this to Crystal when she is ready and no time sooner.'

I knew Leo was hiding secrets from me. But I didn't think he would have a weird box with my name on it. I lifted the box out of the drawer, tore open the flaps, and pulled out what was inside. It was a miniature gold treasure chest covered in a unique spiral pattern. It felt weightless in the palm of my hand.

I was speechless; it was stunning.

There was a knock on the front door, and my chest tightened. I couldn't let myself get caught. I crawled under his bed and slipped the box into my dress pocket.

The front door opened, and Leo stomped inside. I clasped my hands over my mouth. He headed to the bathroom, and I heard running water. I couldn't stay for too long. I rolled out from under the bed and tiptoed towards the door.

"What are you doing?" Leo asked. "How did you get in here?"

Damn, I was so close. I spun around, and he was standing there, shirtless, and blushing.

"Oh, you left the door open. I wanted to talk to you, but it doesn't matter now," I said. "I'll get going."

"Don't act all innocent now. You broke into my room to 'talk' to me?" He put his top back on, marched over to me, and put his hand out. "Hand it over."

I tried to keep a straight face. "Hand over what?"

I couldn't surrender the mini treasure chest. He would make sure I couldn't find it again. I had come this far.

He stared into my eyes. "You know what? Don't play dumb."

"Stop looking at me."

"You can't just dig around in my place, Crystal. I told you to wait."

"But you don't understand how I feel. I'm sick of being in a state of limbo and you won't help me."

"So, you steal from me. If you open that box, you will regret it. Please hand it over!"

"Don't shout at me!" I took the mini treasure chest out of my pocket and opened it.

BRIGHT HALO EPISODE ONE: MELTED MEMORIES

A gush of gold glitter flew into the air and filtered throughout the room. My legs went weak, and I fell forward.

Leo caught me in his arms and cradled me. "Crystal, what have you done?"

I closed my eyes and disappeared into my mind.

Chapter Seven: Don't Lie To Me

I raced down the stairs and mum was in the kitchen, wearing her favourite baking apron and gloves with her hair up in a high bun. She was humming to herself while taking out a tray of fresh bread rolls from the oven and letting them cool on the stove. The warm, sweet, yeasty aroma filled my nose.

"Smile, Mummy, smile!" I screamed, waving my toy camera.

BRIGHT HALO EPISODE ONE: MELTED MEMORIES

"Hey, love." She bent down and widened her eyes. "Is that my necklace? How long have you had that on?"

"Don't know."

"Tell me now. This is important, Crystal."

"Can't remember."

She took the necklace off and pointed at me. "Mummy has to get tough. If I catch you with this again, you'll be grounded forever. Do you hear me?"

"Why are you so mean?" I cried.

She wiped my face with her fingers and gave me a tight hug. "Mummy's sorry, but you are nearly six, so you need to listen."

"I will, I promise."

"Good girl, can Mummy make you feel better?"

I handed her my camera and said, "Can you please take a picture with me?"

She faced the lens towards us, and the flash temporarily blinded me, but I grinned as widely as I could.

The following day, I got up early to play in the garden with my Barbie and Bratz dolls. The sun shined through my window.

When I got downstairs, I pushed the back door, but it wouldn't open. My mum was cleaning the dishes in the sink filled with soapy water and bubbles. I marched over to her and tugged on the back of her skirt.

She kneeled in front of me. "Sorry, honey, but you should stay inside *today."*

"Why? Pretty please."

"I said no, Crystal."

"But you always say my little lungs need fresh air."

"You're not playing outside, end of!"

I woke up lying in Leo's bed, and he was sitting beside me with his hand on my forehead. "Finally, your temperature is cooling down. I was getting worried."

I sat up, moving his arm away. "What happened?"

"You passed out. The chest contained Angelic Glitter called Seraph Dust. It awakens your true self."

The dream woman expressed the same words in my nightmare, but she was talking about my pendant, not a random box.

Could she be communicating with me through my dreams?

Leo stepped out of bed. "What did you see? It wasn't an ordinary dream, was it?"

He was right. It was a buried memory.

The day the locks appeared on all the windows and doors. And the necklace from my past was the same one I received for my birthday. Why did she lock me up for a piece of jewellery?

I shook my head. "Wrong. It was just a dream. You have

BRIGHT HALO EPISODE ONE: MELTED MEMORIES

been lying to me all this time!"

"Be quiet. I'm sorry, okay?" He wrapped his arms around me.

"Don't touch me, you liar!" I shoved him off and rushed out.

If anyone caught me leaving the boys' boarding room area, I would never live it down. I had to get out of there. I dashed through the bright academy hallways and bumped into Kelly.

"What are you doing here?" she asked.

I sighed. "I could ask you the same thing."

"Well, I have a boyfriend, unlike you."

"If you're in a relationship, why are you so obsessed with Leo? If you want him, you can have him."

"So dense. I bet your mother is ashamed of giving birth to you."

I clenched my fists. "Don't mention my mum!"

"Oh, are you going to hit me?" she asked, poking me in the ribs. "She should have had an abortion. You are embarrassing."

"Shut the hell up! You idiot!"

She slapped me across the face. "Don't talk down to me!"

I held my burning cheek.

My mum hit me the same way on my last birthday. I pushed Kelly to the ground and ran off down the hallway. It felt so exhilarating pushing her, but I knew I would regret it later.

RANDELETTA HOWSON

I closed my boarding room door and collapsed into my bed. Maybe Leo was trying to help me, but I couldn't be sure. He could be the actual killer and could have been keeping me at Wonderstate under false pretence. The masked man carried my mother's body away, but Leo could have been an accessory. It wasn't impossible.

He had that suspicious briefcase of money, after all. I didn't know who to trust and I couldn't even trust myself.

My flashback memory of my childhood kept replaying over and over in my mind. It was wonderful to relive the past, but I had forgotten how emotionally abusive and smothering my mother was. She was the definition of a helicopter mum.

After she passed away, she became pristine and pure in my memories. I guess it was the only way to cope with the grief. But now I wondered what else I had blocked out.

What was the reason she had locked me in the house?

Was she aware that the masked man was after us?

I wished I could ask her questions and get answers. I still loved her, even though I didn't understand her.

I pulled out my mother's necklace from my top drawer. I should have never hidden it. It was the most meaningful thing I owned. I needed to find out why my mum gave it to me and why

BRIGHT HALO EPISODE ONE: MELTED MEMORIES

it made her lock me inside our house for over ten years.

As I clipped it around my neck and closed my eyes, I felt closer to her, despite all the things she had put me through.

Chapter Eight: Play Pretend

*A*t lunchtime, the bell rang. The pupils filtered out of class and into the main corridor. Kelly and her girlmates were standing in the corner, and I wanted to disappear. She always wanted to start something. I rolled my eyes and paced past them, hoping she wouldn't see me in the sea of students.

"Oh, here comes the slut," she announced.

I stopped and let the crowd pass by. "What did you say?" I

BRIGHT HALO EPISODE ONE: MELTED MEMORIES

should have pushed her harder when I had the chance.

Torturing me was a game for her.

She marched over to me. "You heard me, and I saw you leaving Leo's room. So gross."

"And what? You're so annoying. Shut up for once."

"Why should I?"

"Because Leo is none of your business."

"Pathetic. So you think he is yours?"

"Yeah, I do. He's my boyfriend, so leave us both alone," I blurted out.

I shouldn't have lied, but I needed to rub that smirk off her face. Someone had to knock her off her high horse.

"Okay, I will believe you for once. Look what I have here." She whipped out her phone from her blazer and showed me the screen. She was playing a video of Leo hugging me in his bedroom, and the camera zoomed in on me. "How about we make a trade? I will remove it from the cloud if you kiss him right now."

"No way. Are you crazy? I'm not doing that. Please, please just delete it."

"Well, you are giving me no choice. If he is your boyfriend, it should be cool."

"That's not the point. You can't just spy on people. What's wrong with you?"

"I don't care what you think. I knew you were fake."

"If I do what you demand, you promise to get rid of it?"

"If not, I will upload it everywhere. You have five minutes."

"Fine, watch." I sighed.

I couldn't be seen online. The masked man was still out there, and if he saw the video, I would be dead. I didn't even have social media.

But what if Leo refused and embarrassed me in front of the entire school?

I had to take that risk and stop Kelly from harassing me and ruining my life. It was emotionally draining, and I couldn't take it.

Leo stepped out of his English classroom, and I raced over to him. It was impeccable timing, and I had to move fast. "Hey. It sounds strange, but I need to kiss you," I muttered.

"Okay."

"Are you sure? Did you hear what I said?"

He nodded. "Yep, I did. I trust you."

I wasn't expecting him to be so willing.

Did he fancy me? Did he care about me?

And now I was kissing him with ulterior motives. I could feel Kelly watching me, and there was no backing out now.

I leaned in close to him, and my lips almost touched his. But I couldn't do it.

If I was going to kiss him, I needed it to be special and for love, not forced through blackmail. It would make our relationship awkward forever, so I pecked him on the cheek instead. Kelly never mentioned where or for how long. I hoped my loophole worked.

Leo smiled, and his cheeks grew red. He looked cute, and his lips were suddenly inviting.

I pulled him out of the door and into the courtyard. "I guess I should explain myself."

Leo laughed. "It wasn't even a proper kiss. I was expecting fireworks."

"Well, we are just friends, aren't we?"

"You tell me. You said you wanted to kiss me."

I gently punched him in the arm. "Shut up. Kelly told me to, okay?"

"Wait, this is about Kelly?"

"Yes. Kelly has a video of us in your room and she said that she would upload it if I didn't kiss you," I said.

"So you kissed me on the cheek? I don't think that's what she meant."

"I know it sounds crazy, but will you pretend to be my boyfriend?"

"Is that what you really want, Crystal?" He leaned in close and put his hand on my cheek.

My heart fluttered. Was he going to snog me?

"I'm sorry Crystal, but we have to break up," he announced, taking a step back. "This just isn't working out."

Kelly and her friends strutted past us, laughing.

I squeezed Leo's hand. "Please don't do this."

"It's for your own good. We're friends, and we have to keep it that way." Leo said, before heading back inside.

Leo had made my life worse. I only kissed him on the cheek. So what was his problem? He didn't have to throw me to the wolves. I just wanted to delete the memory of the past ten minutes, and I didn't even want to think about him or his stupid lips.

Kelly paced over to me and laughed in my face. "Well, you proved me wrong, poor Crystal."

I pulled a fake smile. "Well, I kissed him, and he dumped me."

"I guess he was your boyfriend because there is no way you would embarrass yourself if he wasn't."

"So you'll delete the video now?"

"You believed me? I ain't deleting anything. You're so easy to control," she said, showing the video on her phone being uploaded online. The percentage paused at 97%.

Leo bolted out of the academy building and snatched her phone. "I guess I will have to delete it myself and get the police involved."

BRIGHT HALO EPISODE ONE: MELTED MEMORIES

"Are you kidding me? You don't have to take it that far," Kelly screamed, trying to grab it back, but Leo was way taller than her. "Give it back right now! It was just a joke."

He typed on her phone and then handed it back to her. "I suggest you stop stalking Crystal, or I will break your phone next time."

"Whatever, you suck." Kelly sulked and ran off.

I laughed. "Wow, I can't believe you did that."

"I know you think I'm against you, but I'm not," Leo said.

"What about the cloud? She could have it on her laptop or something."

"I deleted it off her phone. And if she has another copy, I will destroy it."

"What? How?"

"I have my ways. You don't have to worry. Are you okay?"

"I'm fine now and thanks for saving me again."

"What are friends for? I have to speak to Mr Gold before class, so see you later." He checked his phone and hurried off.

I sighed as he disappeared back into the building. How could I be so stupid? I was such a coward. Putting myself in the friend zone. He had even given me permission to kiss him.

But I knew I had done the right thing; I couldn't just give my first kiss away to anyone. I wasn't a girl who got what she wanted. Life was challenging enough. I was simply just trying to survive.

And being vulnerable was not worth the risk. My feelings for him would fade with time. I didn't deserve him, and I knew it. Falling in love was not on the cards for me.

I sneaked into Amber's room to find her sitting at her desk, holding a handwritten letter that read, 'Dear Amber, my true love. I miss you and I look forward to embracing you once again xxx.'

"Who is that from?" I asked, taking a step back.

Amber jumped out of her seat and hid the letter in her top drawer. "What are you doing in here?"

"Sorry, I was trying to scare you," I said, folding my arms. "But you were too busy reading the sweetest love letter ever. So you have a boyfriend, after all."

"You caught me yet again. I lied because the situation is way too complicated to explain."

"You know you can tell me anything. You hid the fact you were a waitress and now this? I thought we were friends."

"Okay, I know it looks terrible, but I have my reasons."

"I will forgive you if you tell me about him."

She smiled and sat on her bed. "Okay, well, his name is Ryan, and he is clever and sweet."

"That is so cute. I wish I had a boyfriend sometimes," I said, sitting next to her.

BRIGHT HALO EPISODE ONE: MELTED MEMORIES

"Isn't Leo basically your boyfriend?" she asked. "He likes you. I can tell. It's so obvious."

"I don't know about that."

If only Amber knew what had happened today. The knot in my stomach grew tighter and tighter. I should have just kissed him on the lips.

What did I really have to lose?

Amber waved her hand in front of my face. "Earth to Crystal. You noticed Leo only pays attention to you, right?"

"Only because he feels sorry for me."

Amber rubbed her chin. "What do you mean? Why would he feel sorry for you, Crystal?"

"It's nothing. I'm going to sleep. Goodnight, Amber." I escaped from her bedroom, gasping for air.

There was no way I could tell her about my mother's death when I couldn't even tell her about my stupid crush on Leo. I was such a hypocrite; I had way more secrets than her.

Chapter Nine: Crystal Clear

*A*ll I could see was darkness, and a woman kneeling on a silver floor. I bent down and combed the curtain of black hair out of her face. Her purple eyes stared at me. She put her hands on my cheeks. "It truly begins, my child," she said with a smile. "Let the pendant be your guide and key. You must return, my love."

"What do you mean?" I asked. "Who are you?"

"Her gift is the key to your home and true self. Please remember my words of guidance."

BRIGHT HALO EPISODE ONE: MELTED MEMORIES

"My mother's necklace?"

"There is clarity coming soon. Hold it close at all times. It will protect you."

"But what's so special about it?"

"Your mum sacrificed her life for it. Follow your instincts and inner wisdom, Crystal. Now you must run."

A figure appeared in a grey cloak and grabbed me by the neck with one hand. I couldn't breathe. A mask covered their lips and nose, and their eyes remained closed. I tried to escape their grasp, but they were way too strong. They lifted me and threw me.

My whole body shook when I landed on the ground. I coughed up blood and wiped my mouth. The figure dragged the woman by her mane into the dark. I ran and caught up with them, and the figure faced me. Their devilish scarlet eyes cut right through me.

I woke up with a start. It was another nightmare. The flower of my necklace was hovering in the air, shining the colours of the rainbow, and I was floating above my bed. I screamed and dropped with a thump. There was a sound of rapid footsteps outside my bedroom, and my door opened.

Amber stood in the doorway. Her hair was up in a messy bun, and she was wearing a robe. "Crystal, what was that noise? Heard a loud bang," she said, rubbing her eyes.

I sat up in bed. "I fell on the floor. I'm such an idiot."

"Oh my gosh, you're clumsy as hell."

"Sorry for waking you up, Amber."

"No worries. Are you okay? Did you see a ghost or something?"

"I'm fine," I lied.

"Okay, I better go back to sleep." She yawned and pulled the door close behind her.

I squeezed my mum's necklace. Had I really floated? I had to believe it was a dream. Magic wasn't real.

My phone vibrated on my nightstand and there were three missed calls and a text from Leo that read, 'We need to talk. Call me asap.'

I cringed at the thought of my lips landing on his cheek. I didn't even know him. He was just a random guy who saved me from a house fire. I switched my phone off.

Whatever he had to say could wait.

Amber was in the kitchen, sporting her white fur coat. "You're up at last," she mumbled, munching on toast, with her mouth wide open.

"Gross," I replied, sitting on the sofa. "I can see the food in your mouth."

BRIGHT HALO EPISODE ONE: MELTED MEMORIES

"You're so over the top. I'm in a rush. What are you doing today?"

"Well, it's my day off, so a lazy day, I guess."

Amber took another bite of her toast. "You're so lucky. You could join me for overtime at the café if you're bored."

There was a knock on the front door and Amber answered it. "What are you doing here?" she asked, opening the door wide.

In the doorway was Leo, with dark bags under his eyes. "I need to talk to Crystal. It's an emergency." He hurried inside and raced over to me.

"I'll let you guys talk in private. Bye," Amber said, slamming the door behind her.

I put my hand on his shoulder. "Are you okay?"

"Well, I have been up all night, but I have something to tell you."

"Take a seat. Do you want a drink?"

"Sure," he said, sitting down on the sofa.

The kettle was still hot, so I poured out a cup of green tea and handed it to him.

He took a sip. "Thanks, it's delicious. What brand is this?"

"Are you serious?"

"What?"

"Stop wasting my time and tell me what you want, Leo. Why did you rush inside here? Are you a lunatic?" I asked, folding my arms. "Are you here to lie to me again?"

"Don't even start. You're the one who kissed me and you're mad because I won't pretend to be your boyfriend. Get over it."

"Oh my gosh, stop acting dramatic and I'm not even upset about that. You helped me out with Kelly in the end. The thing I'm still mad about is-"

"The other night, and your mother's treasure box? That is why I'm here. I found out something significant," he said, pulling out the treasure box from his pocket.

"Why did you bring that here?"

"I researched the Seraph Dust all night and it not only unblocks your memories, but it can also unlock your magical powers."

"What the hell are you talking about? Magic doesn't exist. You really should have a nap. I'm worried about you."

"I'm fine. Look, I'm here to tell you the whole truth now. You felt the energy from the Seraph Dust the other day and now you're wearing that." He pointed to my necklace and stepped closer. "That is a mystical object from the other world."

Chills ran down my spine. "No, it's a necklace my mother gave me. A family heirloom, but not magic."

"What aren't you telling me? You have experienced magic, haven't you?"

"I don't know. Something strange happened this morning,

BRIGHT HALO EPISODE ONE: MELTED MEMORIES

but it was most likely just a dream."

"Tell me what happened. From start to finish."

"I don't want to. I can't trust you."

Leo sighed. "But there are so many things you don't know yet, Crystal. If you don't tell me, how am I meant to help you?"

"Stop trying to help me, then. You just make things extra difficult for me in the end."

"Do you mean that? I don't want you to feel that way. Please, I honestly have sincere intentions and I never want to hurt you."

"I don't care. I'm thankful for all the things you have done for me, but I think we need a break from each other for a while."

"Fine, I'll give you time to process the truth, but I can't wait around forever. If you want to find out the truth about your mother, learn to trust me again." Leo stormed out.

Was my necklace magical? In the dream, the woman said it was my guide and key, but I couldn't let myself fall down that rabbit hole.

I closed the front door and escaped to my bedroom. My eyes landed on my wall calendar; the art project was due the next day, and I hadn't even started. Of course, I didn't remember. My mind had been all over the place that week.

I sat at my desk and pulled out my watercolour painting set. A tidal wave of inspiration rushed over me, and I knew what I had to do.

RANDELETTA HOWSON

Morning sunlight poured through my bedroom window, blinding my eyes. I had stayed up all night. My arms and back were aching. I didn't want to move, and all I wanted to do was jump into bed and sleep forever.

I was regretting the countless decisions that had led me to this state. There was no way I could get to class in this shape. As my eyes were closing, there was a loud knock at my door and Amber came in.

"Oh my gosh, you did it! I can't believe it," she said, staring at my painting. "It's magnificent!"

I yawned. "So sleepy. I don't think I can make it."

"No way, you can't fail now! Get up."

"But I'm too tired."

"No buts! Get ready and I'll sort it out. You finished it. You can at least hand the work in. Get moving."

"Okay, chill out." I forced myself to stand up, and I sleepwalked into the shower.

After I got dressed, my breakfast was waiting for me at the kitchen table. I munched down the cheese bagel and drank the green tea. I needed all the caffeine I could get.

Amber put my art portfolio case and backpack on the sofa. "All sorted."

I raced over to her and hugged her. "You're amazing. Thanks for breakfast and my bags. You're a lifesaver."

"I know. What would you do without me?" She glanced at her watch. "You have five minutes, so hurry. You've got this!"

"Thank you, Amber!" I rushed out the door with my stuff.

I couldn't be late, even if I had to run wildly through the campus.

Chapter Ten: Messy Masterpiece

*S*he was the woman from my nightmares and dreams, with her black wavy hair and intense purple eyes. She had a white background and a wide grin.

Even though she never smiled once, I had to paint an idyllic ending for her. She was a character of my imagination, but she felt so real to me.

BRIGHT HALO EPISODE ONE: MELTED MEMORIES

I drew her.

I painted her.

I created her.

Leo stared at my painting in art class and grinned. "Amazing, Crystal, and you finished it on time. What inspired you?"

I held my hips. "Thank you, and it's none of your business."

The past week was confusing enough, and I didn't need him judging me. I was inspired by such a dark dream, but the portrait brought me peace.

Leo put his hand under his chin. "There is something you should know."

I sat on my stool. "This better be worth it. Go ahead."

"The woman you painted is your mother."

"That's not funny."

He shook his head. "I'm not trying to be. It's complicated, but let me try to explain. Melander is your mum, but this image is her true form… she's an angel from another world."

"Are you serious? And I thought I was the insane one. Please stop."

"I'm telling the whole truth to you, I swear. And I will prove it."

He had lost his mind, and he needed a reality check. My mum was a normal human with flaws. "Quit wasting my time," I said. "Tell your stories to someone else."

"But you can learn the truth about your mother and the intruder who inflicted that mark," he replied.

I stared at the back of my hand. The dark scar had faded over the year, but the memories of the house fire hadn't.

Of course, I was dying to understand my mum and her motives. And get revenge on the masked man.

I had been searching for the truth, but Leo's remarks sounded fictional.

Our art teacher, Mrs Elson, patrolled the classroom and Leo walked back to his seat across the room. I didn't have time to process what he was saying, so I had to ignore his words and act normally. I slipped off my chair and stood next to my painting.

Mrs Elson approached me and viewed my project. "Crystal, this piece is so full of emotion and creativity. Your talent shines through each stroke. I can see how intensely you have worked. Well done."

"Thank you," I said, trying not to smirk.

I wanted to run to the rooftop, and dance and shout. I finished the work and Kelly didn't ruin it. Things were getting better.

"No problem, keep up the splendid job," Mrs Elson replied, scribbling on her clipboard and moving on to the next student.

I caught Leo staring at me, and one second later, he was standing right beside me. "We don't belong in this world, and we must return home," he whispered.

I took a step back from him. "Please stop. You're freaking me out."

The whole classroom stood still, and the students and Mrs Elson froze on the spot. I checked my watch to see that it had also stopped.

"What the hell? Did you just pause time?" I asked, paralysed in fear. "Who are you?"

Leo lifted his hands, and all the paintbrushes flew up into the air, blasting paint all over the classroom. "Do you believe me now?"

I closed my eyes instinctively as wet paint splattered all over my body. "What are you doing? Please stop!" I screamed.

The paint in my mouth was sour. I wiped my face and opened my eyes. Thick colour consumed the entire room, and everyone looked like human rainbows. I couldn't deny magic when I was staring right at it.

Leo had no paint on him. "Please tell me you believe me. I'm trying to help you, but you didn't take me seriously. You have been on Earth for too long."

"If you had this power, why didn't you use it to save my mother and stop her killer that night?" I screamed. "Instead of using it to scare me now."

"Well, I couldn't use it back then. It's complicated."

"You keep saying that! Pretty convenient, huh? It was you who helped the masked man. Tell me the truth, once and for all."

"We have already been through this? I don't know who he is, and I came there that night to save you and your mother."

"Liar! Then why did you carry a briefcase with all that money that night?"

"I just borrowed money from a friend."

"What kind of friend would give you that much cash? You told me you came from a rich family, remember? Are you forgetting all your lies?"

"Stop with all the questions. You are missing the main point of this conversation, Crystal. We need to go back home."

"I'm not going anywhere with you! Leave me alone!"

"You never listen," Leo said, waving his hands.

A pile of chalk and drawing pencils rolled onto the floor. The ruined paintings jumped off the easels and floated into the air.

There was darkness in Leo's eyes, and he aimed the paintings at me. I was stupid for even trying to communicate with a supernatural lunatic.

"Promise me you'll follow my instructions!" he continued.

I wanted to punch him, but he could have thrown me across the room with his powers.

"Yes, yes. I promise!" I shouted. "Just stop this already."

In a blink, the classroom was back to normal. The paintings

BRIGHT HALO EPISODE ONE: MELTED MEMORIES

were untouched, and the walls were crisp white. The students were chatting and laughing again.

On my final art piece was bold red writing that read, 'Meet me tomorrow morning. 6 am at Boldworth Park.'

Then the writing disappeared right in front of my eyes.

Why would Leo want to meet me in a park so early?

What was he planning to do?

Mrs Elson stood behind her desk. "Class is dismissed! Have a wonderful day and well done class."

The lesson was over before it began. An entire hour had passed in fifteen minutes. Could Leo manipulate time and stop it?

Was he even human?

He had vanished, and I wasn't sure what to think. Was he intending to hurt me if I didn't follow his instructions?

There were two things I knew for certain: he wasn't someone to mess with and he definitely wasn't from this world.

Chapter Eleven: Neon Awakening

I stared at myself in my full-length bedroom mirror, wearing a black gown and boots. It was the night of my birthday and the anniversary of my mother's death. I cried alone in the afternoon, remembering my mum's laugh, hugs, and kindness. I hoped she was proud of me.

Amber paraded into my room in her silver dress and heels.

BRIGHT HALO EPISODE ONE: MELTED MEMORIES

"You are slaying, girl. Are you excited about tonight?" she asked, standing beside me.

"Yeah, looking forward to letting my hair down for once."

"You deserve it, Crystal."

"But I'm worried that I might see Kelly there," I said.

I hadn't seen her for a week, and I couldn't relax for a second.

Amber shook her head. "She will be hiding. I heard her parents have gone bankrupt."

"Why am I only hearing this now?"

"You hate gossip, apparently. You'll be fine, I promise."

I smiled at my reflection in the mirror. "Right, I'm going to enjoy tonight, no matter what."

At least I didn't have to worry anymore. Kelly's father no longer had the academy in the palm of his hands.

Amber pulled out a white paper bag from my drawer. "Here, open it."

"Where did you get that? You're a spy." I opened the bag and retrieved a red beaded bracelet. "Oh wow, thank you. It's so gorgeous."

She rolled her right sleeve up and showed her matching bracelet. "I'm not telling you the price. It's a symbol of our friendship."

I slipped on my bracelet and hugged her. "I adore it."

She giggled and pushed me away. "Glad you love it. Now tell

me about the kiss?"

"It was only a peck." I sat on my bed, pulling on my ankle boots.

My stomach flipped just thinking about Leo's powers. I knew ignoring him was a dangerous game.

"Oh my gosh, is that it?" she asked, sitting next to me. "How did he react?"

"He was fine until I told him that Kelly blackmailed me into doing it."

"He thought you liked him. You should ask him out."

"No, I'm cool being single. How's your boyfriend?"

"I am visiting him for summer break." She poked me in the arm. "Tonight will be awesome! Snog Leo while I'm gone."

"No way. I'm just pretending it never happened."

"Why? You fancy him, right?"

"I don't know. Too complicated."

Of course, I liked him.

I couldn't just turn my feelings off like a tap. But after seeing his strange powers and impulsive behaviour in art class, I was glad I didn't give my first kiss away.

Amber's phone vibrated on my nightstand, and a message appeared. "The Uber is here," she said.

"Wait for me, one second." I grabbed my handbag, and we rushed out, with our arms linked.

BRIGHT HALO EPISODE ONE: MELTED MEMORIES

A powerful smell of alcohol hit me as I entered Club Neon, and there was no space to move onto the dance floor. Flashing strobe lights darted around the dim room and music blared from the speakers. A group of girls screamed in the corner, sitting at a booth with an ice bucket, tall glasses, and vodka bottles. The head girl had a badge on her dress that said, 'Birthday Girl.' Was that how normal people celebrated?

Amber pulled me to the bar and spoke to the bartender, but I couldn't hear her over the loud music. The bartender mixed and poured two glasses of a bright indigo cocktail.

"Happy Birthday, Crystal!" she screamed, handing me my drink. "You're eighteen now, so enjoy your drink."

"Thank you." I gulped down my cocktail and winced at the mint mouthwash taste.

"Do you love it?"

"I don't know. What is this?"

"Blue Mojito, it's lovely, right?" she said, finishing her drink.

She ordered six shots of vodka, and we downed them. It was firewater, and I had to stop myself from vomiting.

"I'm not sure I enjoy drinking to be fair," I replied. "Don't think it's for me."

"Don't worry, you just got to find the right drink."

"How long is that going to take?"

"We are only starting the night and drinks are on me. So do you feel different? Being one year older and all."

"The same, really. Well, at least I can drink now, I guess," I said, forcing a smile.

Amber laughed as she stepped away from the bar. "Always a silver lining. I promise you will find your favourite drink tonight."

"I hope so."

"Have I ever let you down?"

"Nope."

The music changed, and Amber screamed. "I love this song!"

She grabbed my hand and pulled me onto the crowded dance floor.

We danced and swayed as if there was no tomorrow, and the songs melted into each other, and we couldn't help but sing along. My worries had drifted away, and the buzz of alcohol had hit me.

After two hours, Amber shouted in my ear. "I'm going to get some drinks, so you stay here." She hurried over to the bar before I could reply.

Why was she leaving me on my own?

I went to join her, but Leo stopped me in my tracks. What was he doing here? He stepped in front of me and moved his face close to mine.

BRIGHT HALO EPISODE ONE: MELTED MEMORIES

"Hey, you look gorgeous tonight," he said.

"Save it, Leo," I replied.

"I know you don't want to talk, but let me buy you a birthday drink."

"And why would you want to do that? You clearly don't even care about me."

"I just need ten minutes of your time."

"Whatever." I crossed my arms. "Fine, you have five minutes."

I settled in a booth in the club's corner, waiting for Leo. I had to hear him out, and I knew if I didn't agree to his request, he would undeniably show me his powers again. He placed two red drinks on the table and sat next to me. "Amber told me you should love this one. Cranberry Juice and Vodka."

I pointed to the other side of the booth. "Shouldn't you be sitting across from me?"

He leaned in and whispered in my ear. "But then you wouldn't be able to hear me properly."

My spine tingled at his deep voice as I grabbed my drink and took a sip. It was sweet and Amber had indeed found me the right drink.

Just wished Leo weren't the one to buy me it.

"Okay, then let's get this over with. What do you want?" I asked.

"I wanted to say sorry."

"What for? Scaring me half to death?"

"But I did it all for a reason and I had to make myself clear. You saw my message on your painting, right?"

"Yeah, I saw it, but there's no way I'm meeting you in the park alone. Just because you're some magical freak. It doesn't mean I have to do what you say, Leo or whoever you are."

"Don't you want to find out the truth about your mother?"

My blood boiled as I grabbed the collar of his shirt and moved closer to him. "Don't you dare bring my mother into this?"

"What are you going to do?" he asked, locking his eyes with mine. His blue eyes pierced through me. "Kiss me?"

He was baiting me, and I wouldn't let him win. He was handsome, but his attitude was trash. "That's never going to happen in a million years."

"Calm down, I'm only joking."

"Well, stop it! I'm tired of this."

"You can't avoid me forever, Crystal."

I let go of his collar and pushed him back. "Whatever, I'm here to have an enjoyable night and that's what I aim to do. So, leave me alone, okay?"

BRIGHT HALO EPISODE ONE: MELTED MEMORIES

"Go on, I ain't stopping you," he said, standing up from the booth.

"Thank you." I jumped up and escaped onto the dance floor.

I entered the empty girls' toilets and washed my hands in the sink, feeling the warm water on my skin. My white nail polish was already chipping and peeling. Nothing was turning out right. Why couldn't Leo leave me alone? He was driving me crazy, and he couldn't even let me enjoy my birthday in peace.

A stall door opened, and Kelly stepped out. "So naïve," she said. "Did you genuinely think I would just let you get away with it?"

I took a step back. "I don't want any trouble, Kelly. Leave me alone. I don't understand why you hate me so much."

"Don't take it personally, but I have orders to follow."

"What do you mean?"

"You're pathetic. Your mum must be rolling in the grave that I buried her in. Don't you remember the day we really met?"

"What are you talking about? Are you saying you killed my mother? Wait, you're the masked man, but how?"

There was no way a teenage girl could be the masked man. She had to be lying, but how would she even know about what happened to me before arriving at Wonderstate?

Unless Leo told her, but why would he do that?

A smile spread across Kelly's face, and she giggled. "Oh impressive, you're finally using some brain cells."

"You're evil!" I stepped closer to her and clenched my fists. "Why? I don't understand! It makes no sense! Who told you to kill her?"

"I guess you'll never know!" She pulled out a gun from behind her back and aimed it at me. "Now, let's get this over and done with. Kiss your life goodbye."

Bang.

Bang. Bang.

Everything slowed down as the three bullets came rushing towards me. I held my hands out and a blast of purple fire rushed out of my palms. The purple fire burned the bullets to ash and sent Kelly flying backwards.

She landed in a sink and the back of her head crashed into a mirror. She slumped forward and blood dripped down her face and stained her cream dress and shoes.

A metallic smell filled the air.

Was she dead?

I stood there, staring at the palms of my hands.

I was numb. This couldn't be happening.

I tiptoed over to her and touched Kelly's arm. She was ice cold and stiff.

BRIGHT HALO EPISODE ONE: MELTED MEMORIES

Who the hell was I and what had I done?

I caught sight of myself in the mirror beside her. Above my head was a golden ring of light. I had to be seeing things.

Magic didn't exist.

I had killed someone, and now I was losing my mind. I burst into uncontrollable tears and collapsed on the bathroom floor.

It all started with fire, and I guess that's how it would end.

Chapter Twelve: Mirrored Red

I was in a living nightmare. Kelly was lifeless in a sink, and her blood was pouring onto the bathroom floor. Her cream dress was charred with a violet tint. It was a sight I could never erase from my mind.

When I heard the door knock, I nearly jumped out of my skin. Before the blood pool reached me, I got to my feet. I pulled my phone out of my handbag, and there was a text from Leo that read, 'It's me. Are you okay?'

Did he have X-ray vision?

I let him inside and the corridor was empty. His eyes widened when he saw the crime scene.

He slammed the door shut and asked, "Is she dead? What happened?"

"She told me she killed my mother and pulled out a gun and I was so scared. Then purple fire came out of my hands. It was an accident, I swear."

"Fire, huh? That must have been your powers. Okay, let's stay calm. You did the right thing."

"This is crazy," I said, holding my head in my hands.

I had taken someone's life and now I was going to rot in prison forever. Kelly was a horrible person, but I never wanted to kill her.

"This is her doing. She made sure there weren't any witnesses. Only we can enter the bathroom, so she must have used a Seal Spell. She planned to murder us from the start."

"I don't understand. This is too much."

"I will explain magic later." Leo picked up the gun from the floor and rinsed it under a tap. "But first, we need to get rid of the evidence."

"But she's dead, and it's all my fault!"

Kelly's eyes fluttered open, and she hopped out of the sink. Her face was grey as she lurched towards us.

How could she still be alive?

Leo grabbed the wet gun and shot at her twice, but she just choked and spat the bullets back at me. I ducked and my feet landed in the pool of blood.

Kelly laughed. "Your luck will soon run out."

"What are you?" I asked.

"Follow me, Crystal," Leo said, taking my hand.

We escaped through the emergency exit into a dark, narrow alleyway. I left bloody footprints on the ground and there was nowhere to hide. The sound of dance music blared through the brick walls. Club-goers were partying inside while we were running for our lives.

We came to a dead-end of a small factory building with a sign that read 'No Entry–Danger.' The metal doorknob was rusty and broken in half.

Leo pushed the door, but it wouldn't budge. "You need to help me!" he shouted.

"What the hell is she? This can't be real," I asked.

"Crystal. This is real life. Do you want to die?"

Why couldn't I move or think straight?

I glanced behind us, and Kelly was getting closer and closer. She leapt into the air and huge, dark wings appeared on her back.

BRIGHT HALO EPISODE ONE: MELTED MEMORIES

I had to act now and save a mental breakdown for later. I pushed and banged on the door with Leo until it broke open.

"Hurry!" Leo said, shoving me inside the dark small room.

He slammed the door shut, and we rested our backs against it as water dripped in the distance. A hanging lightbulb came swinging towards us and exploded into pieces.

"Leo!" I screamed as the shatters of glass hit my feet.

The door banged and pressure from the other side pushed us forward.

"We have no choice." He moved away from the door. "Let go!"

I pushed my back against the door again. "Are you insane?"

He pulled me away from the door into the corner of the room. He embraced me close in the darkness and I wrapped my arms around him. His shoulders were tense, and his soft, warm breath was on my face.

There was another loud bang, and the door smashed open. I held my breath and stood still.

"Where are you two? You think you can hide from me? I will prove you wrong!" Kelly shouted.

She sounded close. The broken glass made a cracking sound under her feet.

Moonlight flooded into the room from the arched door, and Leo let go of me. He outstretched his hands and wiggled his fingers. The electric wire that hung from the ceiling wrapped around Kelly's arms and pulled her into the air. The wire wrapped around her whole body, but her wings broke free.

Kelly's eyes glowed white, and she said, "Let go of me now, you fool. And I might make your deaths less painful. You can't get away from me!"

"I would shut up if I were you!" Leo waved his hands, and the shards of glass flew towards her and stabbed her wings.

"I will kill you!" Kelly let out a blood-curdling scream and tried to wriggle free. The last part of the wire taped her mouth shut.

Leo grabbed my hand, and we ran back into the alleyway. "We need to go to the park."

I let go of his hand and stopped. "Wait. As long as I can see Amber, I will do it."

"Are you serious? Have you got a death wish?"

"I don't care. I might not see her again."

Leo coughed and went pale. "Fine, but we have to hurry."

"Thank you. Are you okay?" I asked, putting my hand on his back.

He nodded. "I will be okay. Let's just go. The wire won't hold Kelly forever."

BRIGHT HALO EPISODE ONE: MELTED MEMORIES

I rushed inside Club Neon and pushed through the dancing crowd. Amber was easy to find. She was alone at the bar, ordering another drink.

I sprinted over and hugged her. "You're safe! I love you so much, Amber!"

Amber giggled. "I love you too, Crystal. How much have you been drinking? Are you okay?"

"Yeah, but I have to go somewhere with Leo. It's an emergency. Sorry about tonight."

"Don't worry. It's fine."

"Promise me you'll get home safe."

"I promise," Amber said. "I will talk to you tomorrow."

I wanted to confess the whole truth to her, but I couldn't tell her anything. It would only put her in danger, and I would look insane, talking about magic and Kelly being a killer. I just hoped she knew how much I appreciated her as a friend. Hopefully, I could call her again in the future when my life was no longer in danger.

I forced a smile and hugged her again. "Goodbye, Amber," I said, holding back my tears again.

Leo's truck was parked on the street across from the club. We climbed inside and put on our seatbelts. Were my birthdays destined to be tragic?

Murder and painful goodbyes. But having my mum's necklace and Leo to protect me was a blessing. He was always by my side, even though I never appreciated it.

"We need to follow the plan and stay calm," Leo said as he drove onto the road.

There was a traffic jam at the end of the main street. He sped through an open alleyway into a side lane.

I jumped forward in my seat. "Freaking hell."

"Sorry, but we can't let Kelly find us. You saw how dangerous she is."

"But we can stop her, right?"

"No, we need to leave as soon as possible."

"I wish we brought Amber with us. What if Kelly tries to hurt her?" I asked, staring at my friendship bracelet.

Amber had given me the perfect present without even knowing it.

"She won't go near her, I promise."

"But you can't promise that."

"I'm fairly sure I can. Kelly can smell the magic on us," he said, pointing at the car's mirror. The reflection showed Kelly flying behind us.

BRIGHT HALO EPISODE ONE: MELTED MEMORIES

Chapter Thirteen: The First Fall

Kelly flew like a dark-winged ballerina in the midnight sky. She was a nightmare in the flesh and had finally exposed the horrible truth. My mother's killer was right under my nose for a year. And here I was, running away again. I wanted to vomit.

The masked man and a petty school bully were flawless

disguises. I would have never figured out her true identity in a million years. And now she had transformed into a demon butterfly with a thirst for blood. What was she capable of?

"We need to lose her and hide," I said, staring out of the car windows. I couldn't take my eyes off her.

"Just chill out," Leo replied.

"How can you be so calm? Do you not see her? Where are we going?"

"There is only one place to go."

"You mean Boldworth Park?"

"That's correct. Hold on tight, Crystal," Leo said, before speeding through red lights and ahead of vehicles on the road.

Car horns beeped and people screamed outside their windows, but nobody noticed Kelly in the sky.

Was she invisible or something?

Nothing was impossible after that night. She was getting close, and she wasn't slowing down.

Leo drove around a roundabout in circles, staring ahead. A lorry sped past, and the driver glared at us.

Kelly flew in front of our vehicle, flapping her wings. "That was a stupid decision, you idiot. You're making this easy," she said. Her voice made my skin crawl, but I agreed with her.

"What are you doing? She is going to kill us. Drive!" I yelled.

Leo braked the car. "Calm down, I have a plan."

BRIGHT HALO EPISODE ONE: MELTED MEMORIES

"Are you serious?"

"Trust me, Crystal, brace yourself!" he shouted, pulling out the gun and shooting through the front window.

Glass shattered through the vehicle as Kelly fell into the middle of the street, face down, with twisted, wounded wings.

"Wait, this doesn't feel right. How did we stop her this time?" I asked, glued to my seat.

"Well, I guess I hit her weak spot, but she'll heal fast," he said, stepping out and leaving the door open.

"No, keep driving. Please, we can't trust her."

"Crystal, I will protect you. Let's move. Would driving over her make you feel safer? Come on." He was acting as if Kelly was an annoying house spider.

"No way, I'm not getting out." I climbed over to the driver's seat and gripped the steering wheel.

I knew Kelly's tricks and there was no way we could defeat her, so I had to save myself.

Leo dragged me out, lifted me in his arms, and raced across the roundabout.

"Let go of me. I ain't a child," I mumbled, as he put me on the pavement.

He rolled his eyes. "You could have fooled me. Are you coming or not?"

"I have no choice. You better not get us killed."

My emotional walls were crumbling, and I couldn't keep fighting him. It was a pointless battle. I had to trust him. He held his hand out and I took it.

With a pounding heart, we marched into Boldworth Park through the steel gate.

I shivered as the wind hit me, and mud squelched under my boots. It would have been smarter to drive to another city, but Leo was a dog with a bone.

He guided me past a fenced playground and into the park's woods area. Bright shooting stars raced down towards the trees and bushes and into a puddle.

My necklace sparkled and flickered silver. "What's happening? What is all this?" I asked.

Leo put his hands on my shoulders. "Follow my words carefully. Close your eyes and imagine a whirlwind among the trees."

"Okay." I didn't have time or energy to argue again, and I had to survive. He had saved my life twice now, so I could at least listen to him for once. So I closed my eyes, and a coloured swirl popped into my mind.

"You can look now," Leo whispered.

I opened my eyes, and a rainbow whirlwind faced us between

the trees. It took my breath away. "No way! Did I really do that?"

"Yes, we must hurry." He pulled me towards the middle oak tree. "We need to climb up and jump into the whirlwind."

I pushed him. "No! Are you crazy? Please stop this. Can't we just run away somewhere else?"

"No, this is the only way. Kelly will find us anywhere we travel on Earth. You'll be fine if you jump. If you want to find out information about your mother, you will do it."

"Of course I do, but how is this meant to help?"

"Your mother could be in the homeland."

"What? But my mother is dead."

"I told you. The woman you painted is her true form."

I sighed. "But what does that even mean? I watched my mother die right in front of my eyes. She's gone."

"But she had magic. She could have escaped death and we don't know what Kelly did when she took her. I will explain when we get there, okay? You need to make your decision now, before it's too late."

I put my hands on my head. "Let me think! This is too much!"

I didn't know if I trusted him, but the pressure was on. Kelly must have healed and woken up by now, so I had to move fast.

And who knew how long the whirlwind would last?

Magic existed, and I couldn't ignore the truth any longer.

We stood on the top branch of the tree, and I didn't even remember climbing up. It was an out-of-body experience. My head was spinning, and I couldn't catch my breath. The playground areas and rivers looked so tiny from up there, and the night was getting crazier by the second.

"Are you ready, Crystal?" Leo asked, balancing on the branch effortlessly.

Feeling lightheaded, I hugged the tree trunk. "No, I can't do this."

"Yeah, you can. You're braver than you think. Trust yourself."

"Please, this makes no sense. There must be another way. I can't."

I could see the whirlwind right in front of my eyes, but I couldn't get my head around actually jumping.

It was suicide.

I was human, after all. I wasn't invincible.

Leo pulled me from the tree trunk. "I'm sorry, but this is the only way. You'll be safe. You need to jump before your chance disappears, Crystal."

"What if I die? I can't do this," I said, wobbling on the branch.

BRIGHT HALO EPISODE ONE: MELTED MEMORIES

The leaves rustled in the wind, and a few drifted down into the whirlwind.

"I'm not a killer. I know this is huge to ask, but this is our ticket home."

"It just doesn't feel right."

Leo smiled. "Trust me, you'll survive. I'll be right behind you, and I'll see you on the other side."

The other side? I didn't appreciate the sound of that. My mind was telling me to get back to safety and my heart was telling me to jump. My body had to fight the fear of death and believe in magic.

I had to focus on seeing my mother again and hugging her close. If she was alive in another world, I had to take a leap of faith and hope that Leo was telling the truth.

Before the voices in my head could stop me, I took a deep breath and leapt off the branch into the unknown. Gravity pulled me down and I became dizzy with colour. The whirlwind wrapped around me, and I disappeared into the darkness.

TO BE CONTINUED...

Check out the sneak peek of Bright Halo Episode Two: Enchanted Eve ♡

Bright Halo
EPISODE TWO: ENCHANTED EVE

RANDELETTA HOWSON

Chapter Fourteen: Return to the Real Homeland

Present Day
Mysagi Holt, Kingdom of Enchanta Divine

T he sky was misty green, and I was lying down on lilac grass, surrounded by an indigo forest. I sat up and inhaled the sweet and warm air. Was I dead and in some kind of rainbow heaven? Leo had tricked me. The last thing I remembered was jumping out of a tree into a colourful whirlwind.

I staggered barefoot across the damp grass and placed my hand on a solid sapphire tree. I wasn't dreaming. It was real. I had landed in a whole different world, and Leo was nowhere in sight. There was no way he would let me fall alone.

Footsteps approached from behind me, and I nearly jumped out of my skin. It had to be him. I knew he wouldn't leave me. I circled the tree and cut my shoulder on a sharp branch. A gush of blood poured down my arm. Feeling woozy, I fell to the ground.

A young fair-skinned woman with red curly hair raced towards me. She was wearing a silver dress that covered every inch of her thin body.

"Please don't hurt me!" I screamed, holding my hands up. She looked angelic, but I had to remember she was a stranger in a strange world.

"Calm down. You're hurt. Let me help you," she said. She smiled at me and put her hand on my wounded shoulder. The pain was non-existent, and the cuts and blood disappeared right in front of my eyes.

"How did you do that? Who are you?"

"My name is Winstaro. It isn't safe to be out in the dark. Many creatures will be interested in your red blood. Come with me." She put her hand out.

My red blood? What colour blood did she have?

A luminous alien green.

I wished Leo has stayed by my side. He would know what to do. I couldn't stay out all night in the wilderness. I had to trust Winstaro. Why would she have healed my shoulder if she wanted to hurt me?

"My name is Crystal. Thanks for saving me," I said. I took her hand and followed her down a path hidden between the trees.

"You're not from around these parts. Where are you from?" she asked.

I didn't know what to say. "Earth."

"Oh, I visited there in my youth." She talked about her trips to Earth as if they were a holiday for her. Where did Leo send me?

"I have been there my whole life."

"Yeah, you're human. Do you wonder what I am?"

"No." I lied. Of course, I wanted to ask, but I didn't want to be rude. "I just want to go back home."

"Well, rest tonight and I can help with that request."

"Really?"

"Yeah, I'm a witch. It will be an easy trick to send you home."

I stopped in my tracks, and my heart raced. "A witch?"

Was I stepping into a trap?

"Don't worry. I know what humans think of us, but we are just alike," she said, smiling back at me. "Some are noble, and some are depraved, but I'm one of the virtuous ones."

I didn't know what to believe at that moment, but I smiled back. Getting on her wrong side was a disastrous idea. I had to risk it and spend one night with a witch.

We reached a grey cottage hidden under two overarching trees. I was stepping into a twisted fairy tale, and I wished I had left breadcrumbs for Leo to find me.

Winstaro opened the front door and held her hand out. "This is my humble home."

"Thanks." I nodded and stepped inside. There was a sofa and a fireplace near the door, and a circular mirror hung on the back wall next to a closed door.

"You can sleep on the sofa tonight. I will create a spell for you to travel back to Earth tomorrow."

"Thank you again," I replied, sitting on the sofa, and staring up at the black ceiling.

"Make yourself at home. Night. Sweet dreams," she said, handing me a blanket from thin air.

She wandered into her room and slammed the door behind her. I settled on the sofa and pulled the blanket over me. At least I had a warm place to sleep in this weird, foreign land, but I couldn't help but worry. I closed my eyes and held my hands together. *I wish to go home, and I wish Leo is safe.*

In the middle of the night, I woke up to see Winstaro staring down at me. Gasping in horror, I pulled the blanket up to my neck.

"What do you want?" I asked.

"Hand it over!" she screamed. "You said you were human, but why do you have that?"

"What are you talking about?" The flower of my necklace was hanging over my dress's collar. It must have fallen out when I was sleeping. I quickly tucked it away.

"You know what I mean!" she continued. "You can't hide it now."

"It's my mother's. Please, just stop."

Her face softened. "Your mother? So you're the daughter that Melander sent away, aren't you?"

"You knew my mother?"

"I gave her the necklace, so it is technically mine. So hand it over."

"I can't give you it back. It's the only thing I have left of her. Please, just let me go."

"You don't deserve that much power!" She blew toxic green breath onto my face and grabbed the collar of my dress.

"No! Leave me alone!" I coughed violently and pushed her

away. "Get off me!"

She had trapped me on the sofa and there was no way I could outpower a witch.

An arrow flew through the window, and the glass smashed onto the floor. The arrow darted towards us, and I rolled off the sofa onto the carpet, screaming.

Winstaro let out a deafening screech and dropped to the floor next to me. I pulled the key off her belt and raced to the front door. I didn't want to be around for the next arrow.

Find out what happens next in:

Bright Halo Episode Two: Enchanted Eve.

Blurb: Crystal and Leo land in the Kingdom of Enchanta Divine. There are rumours that Crystal's mother may be alive and with the help of Leo's friends, they must find a spellbook that could save her mother's life and stop the evil King Kireo, who mercilessly tortures the Kingdom. Are the rumours about her mother true and will they find the spellbook in time before King Kireo catches them?

Thanks for Reading... ♡

Thank you for reading Bright Halo
Episode One: Melted Memories
and I hope you enjoyed
the sneak peek of
Episode Two: Enchanted Eve.

I would really appreciate an honest review on Amazon or Goodreads so new readers can discover & enjoy my books.

Episode One to Five are released
and ready to read.

More Episodes are on their way in 2023!

Check out the current episodes
on the next pages:

Books in this series ♡

Bright Halo is an Episodic

Young Adult Fantasy Book series

with suspense and slow-burn romance.

Follow Crystal on her adventure

of Magic, Murder and Mystery.

Bright Halo Episode One: Melted Memories.

Buy on Amazon

Blurb: Crystal has been hidden from the world her whole life, but things are about to change when her mother gives her a mysterious necklace on her 17th birthday. One tragic night, her mother is killed in a house fire and everything Crystal has known has been turned to ashes. With an unknown killer out to get her next, how will she survive? Who can Crystal trust, especially when it involves a handsome stranger and magic?

Bright Halo Episode Two: Enchanted Eve.

Buy on Amazon

Blurb: Crystal and Leo land in the Kingdom of Enchanta Divine. There are rumours that Crystal's mother may be alive and with the help of Leo's friends, they must find a spellbook that could save her mother's life and stop the evil King Kireo, who mercilessly tortures the Kingdom. Are the rumours about her mother true and will they find the spellbook in time before King Kireo catches them?

Bright Halo Episode Three: Silver Scars.

Buy on Amazon

Blurb: Crystal and Leo must go on a dangerous adventure against new enemies to find the three ingredients for the Zen potion, so they can stop King Kireo's evil plans and save Crystal's mother from the Dark Castle. Will Crystal and Leo be able to survive on their travels and will Crystal finally learn how to control her magic?

Bright Halo Episode Four: Dark Desires

Buy on Amazon

Blurb: Crystal and Leo must face Winstaro, the witch and evil King Kireo, to protect the people they care about. Still inflicted with Silver Scars, Crystal's life is held in the balance, and she has to embrace her magic to fight. Will Leo and Crystal be able to stop the witch in time and will Crystal survive long enough to save her mother from the King?

Bright Halo Episode Five: Mirror Mind

Buy on Amazon

Blurb: Crystal and Leo face new challenges when they receive a letter from Crystal's mother, speaking of The Otherside. They must travel to the new world before King Kireo reappears. However, Crystal is haunted by the death of Winstaro, knowing her witchy powers are in her veins. Will Crystal and Leo discover how to get to The Otherside? Is King Kireo really in a coma and is Winstaro really dead?

A New Young Adult fantasy Series begins 23rd May 2023: Tarot Princess

Blurb:
Princess Mina is set to marry Prince Aston and become the future queen. Nevertheless, her true wish is to follow in her mother's footsteps to become a tarot reader and heal the world outside. But witchcraft is forbidden in the kingdom by her father, and she isn't permitted to leave the castle.

On the anniversary of her mother's death, Princess Mina is visited by her mother's ghost and is told a shocking secret. Will Princess Mina obey her royal duties and marriage, or will she risk it all for magic and truth?